LIFEBOAT!

In a holiday resort on the Lincolnshire coast at a Bank Holiday weekend the last thing Iain Macready, coxswain of the lifeboat, wants is a spate of hoax calls. But he and his crew have to deal with these just as they have to answer the genuine calls that inevitably come at holiday time. When a storm breaks over Saltershaven, Macready's own daughter is missing at sea in a sailing dinghy, whilst duty obliges Macready to set course away from the area where she may be to answer a distress call from a coaster.

LIFEBOAT!

LIFEBOAT!

by
Margaret Dickinson

Magna Large Print Books
Long Preston, North Yorkshire,
England.

British Library Cataloguing in Publication Data.

Dickinson, Margaret
   Lifeboat!

   A catalogue record for this book is
   available from the British Library

   ISBN 0-7505-0784-5

First published in Great Britain by Robert Hale Ltd., 1983

Copyright © 1983 by Margaret Dickinson

Published in Large Print March 1995 by arrangement with
Darley Anderson.

Magna Large Print is an imprint of
Library Magna Books Ltd.
Printed and bound in Great Britain by
T.J. Press (Padstow) Ltd., Cornwall, PL28 8RW.

00118992

With the deepest admiration this book is respectfully dedicated to the Coxswain, Crew and Launchers of the Skegness Lifeboat, the *Charles Fred Grantham*.

Acknowledgements

I would like to express my sincere gratitude to the three people who gave so generously of their time and expert knowledge in reading and correcting the technical errors in the typescript: Ken Holland, Coxswain/Mechanic, Skegness Lifeboat; William Hill, Instructor, Trent Valley Gliding Club Ltd, and Fraser Lane, Commodore, Skegness Sailing Club.

My thanks also to my husband, Dennis, for his constant encouragement.

Without their help this book could not have been written.

M.D.

Skegness, 1983

CHAPTER 1

At 0600 hours on the Saturday of that August Bank Holiday weekend a small secondary depression of one thousand millibars formed off the coast of Newfoundland and began to move eastwards across the Atlantic.

Iain Macready, coxswain of the Saltershaven lifeboat, was a worried man.

It had nothing to do with the North Sea, nor with the lifeboat, nor even with the approaching August Bank Holiday weekend which would bring the inevitable glut of rescue calls along the stretch of coastal water off the Lincolnshire holiday resort.

The thing—or rather the person—on Macready's mind was his daughter, Julie.

She was standing opposite him now across the breakfast-table, her curly brown hair still ruffled from sleep, her cheeks a little pink. 'Dad, try to like him—for my sake. Please.'

Macready sighed. 'Och, I've nothing

against the laddie, but he—he doesna fit in here with us. Not with his city gent's suits and his father's country estate and his fancy car...'

The pink tinge in her face deepened. 'Dad! That's inverted snobbery if ever I heard it. He's a student—just like me.'

'No, hen, he's no' like you,' Macready said softly.

There was an uneasy silence in the neat, bright kitchen broken only by the rattle of the cups in their saucers as Julie pulled them towards her to pour the tea. Father and daughter avoided meeting each other's eyes.

Macready moved restlessly, his bulk making the kitchen chair creak in protest. 'It's no' that, Julie.' He laid down his knife and fork and eased a sliver of bacon from between his teeth with his thumbnail. 'It's no' that, but we're plain, down-to-earth, ordinary folk and...'

The phone extension on the wall shrilled and Macready, almost welcoming the interruption, was on his feet and lifting the receiver before it could ring a second time.

'Macready.'

'Mac.' It was Bill Luthwaite, the

12

lifeboat's honorary secretary speaking. 'The coastguard's just rung me. He's had a call about a sighting of red distress flares on the mud flats south of Dolan's Point.'

There was an unusual hesitancy in the secretary's voice. Macready, quick to notice it, asked, 'Where did the call come from?'

'That's just it,' Bill Luthwaite's tone was troubled. 'It was anonymous. No name, no details, nothing.'

'Except the message that there's a boat in trouble?' Macready said.

'Yes. Jack—' Bill referred to Jack Hansard, the local coastguard—'has a hunch it could be a hoax, but he would like us to treat it as an anticipatory call out. He's on his way to the area now to take a look.'

'Right. I'll have the lads stand by,' Macready replied. 'I'm away to the boathouse now.'

'Right you are. I'll ring you there as soon as I hear any more from Jack.'

Macready dropped the receiver into its cradle and made for the door. Briefly he glanced back at his daughter still standing beside the table in her pale blue dressing-gown and slippers, the teapot in her hand ready to pour his tea.

'Sorry, hen...' It was more than just an apology for leaving the half-eaten breakfast she had cooked.

Julie grinned impishly. 'Och, away with ye!' She mimicked his brogue to perfection, although there was not a trace of it in her own speech.

Macready grinned, his weathered face creasing into a dozen laughter lines. 'See you later, hen,' he added, relieved that the constraint between them was gone.

When Macready had reached the boat-house, he had only just managed to call up his second coxswain, Fred Douglas, and bowman, Phil Davis, to warn them to be on stand by, when a further call came through from the secretary. 'Jack's down at the Point and he's seen a red flare go up now.'

'That settles it then.'

'Yes. We'll go ahead and launch.'

As Macready rang off and then lifted the receiver and began to dial another number, Phil Davis poked his head round the door of the office. 'What's on, Mac?'

'Red flares off the mud flats beyond Dolan's Point. Would ya fire the maroons for me, Phil, while I ring the rest of the lads?'

Pete Donaldson set the breakfast-tray down on the bedside table next to his sleeping wife and grinned down at Angie's tousled head. That Saturday morning Pete and his wife of five months had planned a lie in—a long lie-in!

He got back into the bed and moved over to her side. His forehead against hers, his knees crooked to meet hers, he gently traced the swell of her breast with his fingers and said softly, 'Tea is served, m'lady.'

Angie opened one eye. 'Thank you, Jeeves,' and as he tried a bolder caress, she added, 'That will be *all*, Jeeves.'

'Angie?'

She closed her eye. 'I'm asleep.' But he could see the mischief twitching her lips even as she spoke.

He moved closer. 'You know what you are, don't you? You're...'

There was a loud crack somewhere in the distance. Pete's whole body stiffened and he raised his head. Angie's eyes flew open instantly. They looked at each other.

'Was that the...?' But he never finished the question for at that moment the green telephone on his bedside table rang. Before

15

it had finished its first peal, he had picked up the receiver. 'Yes? Right. I'll be there.'

In one swift, lithe movement he was out of bed and reaching for his clothes as they heard the bang of the second maroon.

'It's a service,' he told his wife unnecessarily, hopping on one foot whilst he pulled on his trousers. 'They pick their bloody moments, don't they?' He grinned ruefully, grabbed his thick sweater and an extra pair of socks and bent to kiss her quickly.

He thrust his feet into his shoes and was moving towards the bedroom door when Angie raised her tea-cup to him. 'I'll keep it hot for you, love,' she said impishly.

'You do that, darlin',' his voice came back to her as he pounded down the stairs. 'You do that. I'll be back...'

The door slammed and she heard the rattle of his old bicycle as he flung himself on to it and pedalled furiously up the street.

In silent, secret ritual his bride let her eyes stray to the patch of clear sky visible through their bedroom window.

'God keep him safe,' she whispered. 'And bring him back to me.'

The prayer, her own private talisman,

16

said, she drank her tea and then snuggled down beneath the duvet.

She was asleep again before Pete reached the boathouse.

The first maroon had been fired at 08.36 and the second a few moments later. The puffs of green smoke from the maroons were still hanging in the sky above the boathouse when Pete arrived, breathless but still running. Coxswain Macready was in the tiny office at the side of the station making last-minute checks and phoning through to inform Coastal Rescue Headquarters at Breymouth on the Norfolk coast that the Saltershaven lifeboat was about to be launched. Fred Douglas, the second coxswain, was with Macready in the office, and his son, Tony, the signalman, was already aboard the lifeboat where it sat on its launching carriage permanently coupled to the tractor which would tow it to the sea. Saltershaven had a large tidal range and even at high water there was a wide stretch of soft sand to negotiate before the boat reached the sea.

Pete pulled on his sea-boots over his

thick woollen socks, then the stiff orange-coloured oilskins and insulated jacket and the life-jacket. Lastly on went the bump hat—the regulation hard helmet-like piece of headgear. Pete climbed the ladder on to the boat.

'Here, Tony, mate, hook my belt up, will you? What's on, d'you know?' he added as he turned his back and stood patiently whilst Tony Douglas fastened the hooks on Pete's life-jacket.

'Red flares down Dolan's Point way.'

Footsteps pounded across the concrete forecourt of the boathouse and Chas Blake, the emergency mechanic, and Alan Gilbert, the assistant mechanic, arrived together. The head launcher and one of the two tractor drivers were already in the boathouse making ready for the launch so that left only a few more launchers to arrive.

'Right the other end of the town, I was,' Chas Blake panted, but he did not waste a precious second in climbing aboard.

'Aye, an' they pick their bloody moments,' Pete grinned.

There was a knowing chuckle from Fred Douglas. ' 'Ee's still got 'is pyjamas on! Interrupt summats, did we, Pete? That poor lass of yours mun be thankful to hear the maroon go!'

'Not Angie,' Pete laughed. 'She's...'

Whatever he had been going to say was drowned by the vibrating noise which filled the boathouse as the tractor engine burst into life and smoke swirled upwards into the rafters. The huge sliding doors of the lifeboat station, facing seawards, had been folded open and the tone of the tractor engine heightened as it tugged at the launching carriage with its load of some ten tons.

Saltershaven's lifeboat, the *Mary Martha Clamp,* emerged from the shadows of the boathouse. On board, the signalman, Tony Douglas, raised the radar mast as soon as the boat was clear of the doorway, then he made his way along the deck to the bows and proceeded to stow the rope fenders.

Turning left out of the boathouse the tractor quickened pace along Marine Esplanade, the caterpillar tracks rattling loudly on the tarmacked road surface. Several paces in front of the tractor Macready walked with Fred Douglas, his second coxswain, heading the whole colourful procession: the blue tractor

19

and the blue, white and orange lifeboat with three crew aboard and alongside, keeping pace, were the remaining two crew members all dressed in their vibrant orange oilskins and life-jackets with the black lettering RNLI. Walking alongside the boat, too, were the launchers in yellow oilskins and thighboots, and Bill Luthwaite, the honorary secretary, who was accountable for the boat whilst it was on land. Once in the sea the lifeboat became Macready's responsibility.

The road traffic was temporarily halted by a police constable so that the procession could take the quickest, right-hand turn around the fountain in the centre of the crossroads and turn due east on to Beach Road. At the end of this road, the tractor lumbered into the soft sand, the stretch of the beach never washed by the sea in summer. Following the lifeboat now were a smattering of interested spectators who always seemed to gravitate towards the drama of the launching of the lifeboat. Had the service been later in the day, the whole route from boathouse to the sea would have been lined with onlookers, but at this hour of the morning—breakfast-time—only a few witnessed the launch.

Some distance away the council's men were already at their task of clearing away yesterday's rubbish: broken glass, discarded cans, paper bags, dropped ice-cream cones and candyfloss squashed into the sand.

The tide was just on the ebb after standing for about an hour at high water. The tractor and trailer gained the narrow stretch of harder sand, still wet and virgin from the retreating waves, and arrived at the water's edge. The tractor turned parallel to the sea, paused whilst the small trailer towed at the rear of the bigger carriage was unhitched and then continued in a wide arc to bring the lifeboat pointing, bows first, out to sea.

On the top floor of a block of holiday flats, quite close to the lifeboat station, the sound of the first maroon had awoken Nigel Milner.

He lay a moment in that strange state somewhere between sleep and full wakefulness, not sure whether he had really heard a noise or whether he had dreamed it. Then the second maroon aroused him fully. He rolled off the lower bunk and padded to the window overlooking the esplanade.

21

The twin puffs of green smoke from the maroons drifted seawards, but the boy from the Midlands did not understand their significance.

Then, far beneath the window, he saw a man running along the pavement and another pedalling his bicycle along the road. They both turned into the lifeboat station, the man on the bike flinging it carelessly against a wall in his haste.

'Hey, Martin, there's summat goin' on at t'lifeboat place.'

Awkwardly, for he was an overweight ten-year-old, Nigel stood on the lower bunk and shook his younger brother's shoulder. 'Come on, let's go an' 'ave a look-see. Come *on!*' He gave the thinner boy's arm a vicious pinch.

'Gi' ower,' Martin murmured and rubbed his arm, his eyes still closed, his head still buried in the pillow.

But Nigel was determined. He dragged the loose covers from the younger boy, who turned over quickly, made a grab for the disappearing bed-clothes, missed and fell out of the top bunk on to the hard floor.

He began to snivel. 'Mam, Mam, it's our Nigel, he's...'

'Ssh!' The fat boy bent over him. 'Don't waken them up—they'll not lerrus go.'

Martin's whimpering stopped and he looked up into Nigel's pudgy face. 'Go? Go where?'

'To watch t'lifeboat. Come on.' Roughly Nigel grabbed Martin's arm and hauled him to his feet. 'Get dressed,' he ordered, reaching for his own shorts and tee shirt. 'We don't need no shoes.'

Ten minutes later—fifteen after the maroon had first awoken Nigel—they were standing at the end of the road leading on to the sand.

'There it is,' Nigel pointed and, without waiting for agreement or otherwise from his brother, he set off after the lifeboat, following the deep ruts made by the tractor and trailer right across the soft sand.

As the two boys raced across the beach, the tractor released the launching carriage, pulled forward and swivelled around on its own axis, churning the sand, and was then re-coupled. The rest of the crew climbed aboard, Macready last, and a launcher removed the ladder. Macready fastened the safety chain across the opening and the tractor pushed the carriage and boat into the sea until the caterpillar tracks were completely hidden by the water. The four restraining chains were released from the sides of the boat when Macready blew his whistle and the launching gear was operated by the tractor driver. The lifeboat slipped from its carriage into the waves, the seawater at once flooding into her ballast tanks and then, engines revving, the *Mary Martha Clamp* headed out to sea.

Nigel Milner gripped Martin's stalk-like arm. 'I say, let us play lifeboats. I'll be t'captain.'

Scornfully Martin said, 'T'ain't "captain", 'tis coxswain!' He pronounced it "cockswane". 'I seen it in that guide book they got at the flat.'

'Oh Clever Dick.' Nigel punched Martin's arm again.

'Gerroff! 'Sides, we can't. We can't blow us dinghy up.'

'Don't need to.' Nigel leant towards him excitedly. 'Don't you remember? Last night we was late back from the beach and Mam was werritin' about bein' late for t'bingo. Well—Dad never let the dinghy down!' He delivered the last sentence like a coup de grâce and stood back to watch Martin's expression. But the enthusiasm he had anticipated was not forthcoming.

'They'll be mad,' Martin volunteered. 'That's why he lets it down ev'ry night, so's we won't go playin' in it by us selves.'

'Baby Buntin'.' Nigel said scathingly. 'Who's chicken then? Look the sea's as calm as anything.' He waved his fat arm in the direction of the ocean.

They looked. The sea was indeed calm, the morning mist still shrouding the water's edge in secretive patches, mist that heralded another hot day—the last of their holiday. Nigel's next manoeuvre was to remind his younger brother of this fact. 'Won't 'ave another chance this year,' he said slyly. 'By the time me dad gets up, it'll be time to pack up an' go for t'train home.'

Back to dusty grey streets and concrete playgrounds without a drop of salt water or a grain of sand.

Martin hesitated, wavered and was lost. 'Come on, then.'

They raced across the beach, sand showering from their flying feet.

Behind them, deceptively benign, the sea lay in wait for the innocents.

CHAPTER 2

As the lifeboat chewed its way through the shallows towards the open sea, Timothy Matthews stood watching the boat he had just helped to launch and feeling the inevitable twinge of longing, that peculiar 'left-behind' feeling he always felt as he watched the lifeboat out of sight.

Tim could not remember a time when he had not been at the water's edge, or very near it, at a launch. Not always as a launcher, of course; only comparatively recently had he been old enough to take an active part. But no one had ever been able to stop him being there watching, longing to go with them, waiting to grow up...

As he turned from the shoreline, he saw the two boys and it was like a ghostly reminder of his own childhood. Only now there were two of them and there had only ever been one of him.

Tim had always been a loner.

He paused a moment to study the two boys. The fat one was talking urgently to the smaller one, bending towards him, bullying him almost, it seemed to Tim. Then they turned and ran across the sand.

Tim smiled and shook his head wonderingly. He glanced over his shoulder at the lifeboat, a hazy shadow through the patchy sea-mist, but still visible.

That was where any similarity between him and the two boys ended.

Timothy Matthews would never have left the beach until the lifeboat had been gone completely from sight for at least ten minutes.

No one had ever been able to stop him. His house-father in the Home, his teachers at the local grammar school, even the headmaster who was feared by many a would-be truant, all had been helpless when confronted by the boy's obsession.

The instant the maroons sounded, Tim had been away to the boathouse, leaving meals unfinished, lessons, the football field—to the cries of anger from his friends if he were in goal. He would even leave his bed in the dormitory of the Children's Home where he had lived since babyhood. Nothing and no one could deter him from being present every time the lifeboat was launched. Since the age of seven, he had only missed one launch and that had been because he was in hospital under sedation on the operating table losing his tonsils.

Even ordinary childish illnesses had not deterred him. On different occasions he had appeared at the boathouse covered in chicken-pox blemishes, measles and an out-of-shape mump-swollen face. Once, during a nasty bout of 'flu, the only reason he had escaped pneumonia was that his housemother had followed him in her car and then he had only been persuaded to get into the car if she promised to follow the lifeboat to the beach and park as near as possible so that he could watch the launch.

All punishment failed. Neither canings, nor detentions, nor early-to-bed had any effect. As soon as the maroon sounded there was no stopping him. Even a car back-firing was enough to make him leap to his feet.

'Bend over, Matthews,' the headmaster would say with resignation.

'Yes, sir. Do you know, sir, it was the fastest launch this year? I timed it. Twelve minutes, forty-five seconds.' (Whack) 'It's a member of the crew of a trawler, sir,

he's got an appendicitis that's gone wrong.'
(Whack)

'Peritonitis.' (Whack) The headmaster
supplied the information along with another stroke.

'That's it, sir. That's what he's got. I
reckon,' (Whack) 'they ought to call in
the helicopter from the airbase.' (Whack)

'I'm sure the coxswain will take heed of
your advice, Matthews.' (Whack)

The headmaster turned away, but the
boy had not finished even if the caning was
done. He stood up, his eyes shining, the
ready smile still on his mouth. 'Oh, he's
a great coxswain, Mr Macready. Eighty-
seven lives he's saved in the eleven years
since he's been coxswain. It's all up on a
board in the boathouse, sir...'

'Yes, yes, that will be all, Matthews.
Return to your class.'

Only now, in the face of the headmaster's
lack of interest in the town's lifeboat
activities, did the boy's expression alter.
Tim could not understand how anyone,
particularly the headmaster who was always
exhorting his pupils to take a lively interest
in whatever was going on around them,
could not be as enthusiastic as he was
about the lifeboat.

The headmaster sighed as the door closed behind Matthews. 'Doesn't anything have an effect on that boy?' he murmured.

The school's secretary, typing in her corner, glanced at him, pursed her lips and said nothing but pounded the keys even harder. Mrs Hibbett did not agree with punishing young Matthews. She thought the boy showed spirit.

The next time Matthews stood in front of Mr Edwards, the headmaster said, 'Well, boy, so it's happened again, has it?'

'Yes, sir. Do you know, sir, they were a crew member short. If only I'd been older perhaps they'd have let me go.'

Mr Edwards raised his eyebrows and murmured, 'Heaven forbid!' Clearing his throat he added, 'Well Matthews, caning seems to have no effect. I—er—understand you particularly dislike the writing of essays. Is that correct?'

The boy grimaced. 'Yes, sir.'

'Well, then. I suggest you remain in detention after school this evening and write me out a full account of the launch of the lifeboat and why you feel the crew have especial need of your presence *every* time a launch takes place.' The sarcasm was lost on Tim. His eyes were shining. 'Yes, sir.'

As the door of his study closed behind a jubilant Matthews, Mr Edwards remarked to his secretary, 'Mrs Hibbett, I think I have just been outmanoeuvred.'

She said nothing but smiled down at her typewriter.

The essay had been a brilliant piece of prose from the fourteen-year-old boy and was passed amongst the staff as an example of what Matthews was capable of achieving.

'If only they put a question in the G.C.E O-level paper about lifeboats,' remarked his English teacher wryly, 'he'll get a distinction!'

Throughout his boyhood Tim had always been welcome at the Macready home. Mary Macready had been like a mother to him. She had never fussed over him—she hadn't been that sort of woman, but he had loved her for her serenity, her smile, her warmth.

Her sudden death had left Tim Matthews every bit as desolate as her husband and daughter.

They had grown up together—Tim and Julie Macready. They had gone to Saltershaven Grammar School, though Julie, a year older than Tim, had been in the form above him all the way through the school.

In their early teens they had gone sailing together, roller-skating, ten-pin bowling, and played tennis. And they could not count the number of times they had waited together for the lifeboat to come back from the sea.

Julie had grown from a spotty, gawky school-kid into a pretty college student and now, at this Bank Holiday weekend, Tim was two weeks past his eighteenth birthday and had just received the results of his A-level examinations. The cheeky boyish grin was still there, the springy fair hair and the brilliant blue eyes. He was tall and thin and slightly round-shouldered after months of swotting—a defect which was likely to be quickly rectified by his chosen career. His obsession with the local lifeboat had grown into a love for the sea and in a few weeks he was due to join the Royal Navy. So this weekend held a kind of poignancy for him. It was the end of an era in his life, the end of being there whenever the lifeboat was launched. The end of his easy friendship with each and every member of the crew, who had come to regard him as a kind of talisman.

Was it to be the end too of his friendship with the Macready family? He would come back, of course, but could it ever be quite the same again?

'What is it this time?'

She was standing in the open doorway of the empty boathouse as the launchers, Tim amongst them, manoeuvred the heavy trailer back into position to await the recall when the lifeboat was ready to beach.

'Hi, Julie.' Tim moved towards her. 'They're not sure. Bill Luthwaite and Jack Hansard thought at first it could be a hoax call, but then the coastguard saw a flare down Dolan's Sand way, but they've no idea yet what it is.'

Julie pulled a face. 'Oh, one of those. Then there's no knowing what time he'll be back.'

'No. I say—shall we go sailing tomorrow? Sandy would lend us his boat. I'm off in a couple of weeks, you know, so there won't be many more times when...'

'Oh Tim, I'm sorry. I can't. Is it so soon you go?'

'Yes—the fourteenth of September.'

'I am sorry. I'd have loved to have gone—really, but I've got this friend

33

coming down for the weekend. Someone I met at college.'

Knowing it to be an all-girls' college Julie attended, Tim blundered on, 'Well, she wouldn't mind, would she? I mean, we could all three go, couldn't we?'

There was a pink tinge to Julie's cheeks and she avoided Tim's gaze. 'It's not a she—it's a he. He goes to the university adjoining our campus.'

'Oh. Oh, I see,' Tim said flatly.

There was an awkward silence between them, a constraint that had never been there throughout their childhood friendship.

With the toe of his training shoe, Tim scuffed at the little heap of sand that had blown up against the boathouse door.

'Well then, I'd better be off to the shops,' Julie murmured. 'I'll—er—see you again before you go, Tim.'

'Yes. Yes, of course.' He tried to smile, but for once his cheery grin was difficult to summon.

He watched her walk away from him. 'Lucky sod!' he muttered to himself of the unknown undergraduate, then he turned and went back into the boathouse.

The two Milner boys dragged the orange-and-black inflatable from the square of back-yard behind the holiday flats. It was approximately six feet by four feet in heavy-duty PVC with paddles and five buoyancy compartments and blown up by means of a 12-volt inflator.

Across the road they carried it, struggling and awkward, between them. Down the concrete steps and through the sunken gardens along the foreshore, past the bowling-greens and up again over the low sand-dune and across the promenade and down on to the beach itself. Reaching the sand they dropped it and towed it by its grab rope, slithering behind them towards the sea.

No one saw them go—at least no one who could foresee the danger. The coastguard was occupied on the radio link to the out-going lifeboat; the beach cleaners were too busy, their heads down searching for broken glass and sharp tin cans. The beach life-guards had yet to come on duty and no one amongst the smattering of tiny figures on the wide expanse of beach took any notice of the two small boys intent upon their own game: not the man with his metal-detector, nor

35

the woman walking her dog, nor the two other children constructing a dam.

By the time Nigel and Martin Milner reached the shallows they were obscured by the lingering wisps of morning sea-mist, hidden from the watchful eye of their parents—had their parents been awake to be watchful—and out of sight of the vigilant coastguard. They were alone in a make-believe world of their own creation with only the enticing whisper of the sea to lure them on.

They played for some time in the shallows, bouncing in and out of the dinghy, carried to and fro by the waves running up the beach and then receding. They pretended to launch their dinghy— just like they had seen the lifeboatmen do. Martin already aboard, Nigel pushed the dinghy out beyond the breakers and flung himself into the craft. Bobbing and drifting, they played their game, confident that the waves breaking on to the sand would carry them back to the beach.

They did not realise that though the surf carried them towards the sand, each time the ebb pulled them a few inches further and further out to sea.

They could not have chosen a more

dangerous set of circumstances. The time—
two hours and thirteen minutes after high
water—was the very point when the ebb
was at its strongest. The patchy morning
mist hid them from the view of anyone on
the beach or promenade. To make matters
worse, a light, offshore breeze began, gently
at first and then with increasing strength,
blowing away the mist but pushing the
dinghy further and further out to sea...

The time was 09.55.

CHAPTER 3

Saltershaven was a seaside holiday resort
on the Lincolnshire coast. Its resident
population of twenty-three thousand could
be more than trebled during the summer
months. The hotels, guest-houses and
holiday flats which lined the promenades
along the sea front and many of the roads
leading from the town to the foreshore;
the chalets, the caravans and tents—all
catered for over twenty thousand people
staying in the town at the height of the
holiday Season.

The words 'The Season' were as familiar to the residents of Saltershaven as they had once been to the Society World of London in a bygone era—but with a very different meaning. For those directly involved with the holiday trade, the Season meant a long day often beginning before dawn and certainly never ending before dusk. The cafés, the cinema and theatres, the snack-bars, the gift-shops, the amusement arcades; the foreshore with its putting-greens, bowling-greens, kiddies' corner, boating-lake, and paddling-pools; the swimming-pool with its chalets; all catered not only for the visitors who came to stay for a week or two, but for the thirty thousand or more people who visited the resort daily by car, coach or rail. All needed to be catered for—to be fed, to be entertained and sometimes to be protected in an unfamiliar environment. The city child let loose on a wide expanse of beach with an endless supply of sand and water at his disposal was vulnerable.

Innocence and ignorance—the two ingredients most calculated to court disaster.

At the moment when the Milner boys' inflatable began to be pulled away from the shore by the ebbing current off the central beach at Saltershaven, seven nautical miles away the *Mary Martha Clamp* reached the area between the Inner Dog's Head sandbank and the coastal marshland of Dolan's Sand at the northern end of the St Botolphs Deeps. Coxswain Macready throttled back from full speed of eight and a half knots to a cruising speed of about six and a half, and began the methodical zigzagging pattern of reconnaissance.

Macready screwed up his eyes against the glitter of the morning sun on the sea. He noticed with a grunt of satisfaction that the crew had taken up their positions. Phil Davis, bowman, in the bows, and Pete Donaldson, radio/telephone operator, had squeezed himself into the narrow seat and was hunched over the small radar screen which crackled and blipped. He was speaking now to the Coastal Rescue Headquarters at Breymouth on the Norfolk coast on Macready's direction.

'Breymouth coastguard, this is Saltershaven lifeboat. We have reached the suggested area of search. Proceeding on a southerly course adjacent to Dolan's Sand and Haven Flats. Over.'

'Saltershaven lifeboat, this is Breymouth

coastguard. Message received and understood. Out.'

Jack Hansard's voice came on to the radio/telephone. 'Saltershaven lifeboat, this is Saltershaven mobile. Message copied. Out.'

'Pete,' Macready butted in. 'Ask Jack if he's seen any more flares or received any further reports.'

'Right, Mac.' Pete repeated Macready's questions but the coastguard's response was negative.

The other members of the crew had stationed themselves at various points around the boat—each facing a different direction, each scanning his particular expanse of sea as the boat turned and turned again. All of them settled themselves for a time of concentrated vigil.

Macready's hands rested easily on the wheel, sure and steady, as he guided the *Mary Martha Clamp* through the maze of sand banks on the western coast of the Wash. He knew this area so well now, better than the place of his birth.

Iain Macready had been born on Clydeside in the early nineteen-twenties, the son of a shipyard worker and a gentle-eyed kitchen maid. His father had been killed in an accident at work and his mother had died of influenza. So it had been left to his paternal grandmother to bring up young Iain. They had lived in a two-up, two-down terrace house, a street away from the docks, and dockland had been young Macready's playground. His memory of his grandmother Macready, widowed by the First World War, was of a small, thin woman, dressed in an ankle-length black dress, with bright ebony buttons down the front of the bodice. Black ebony earrings dangled from her pierced ears and her grey hair was always stretched tightly back from her face into a bun at the back of her head. Her normal expression had been one of severity, but her lively sense of humour had often softened the lines of her face and made her dark eyes twinkle and her thin mouth quirk with amusement.

It had been a strict up-bringing for the boy, yet a happy one. It was not until years later that he realised just how hard his grandmother had had to work as a housekeeper in a smarter part of the town to give him the security he had then taken for granted. Her pride would not let her accept charity and that same stiff-necked pride had kept the young Iain in ignorance of the long hours she must have worked, for her own home had been spotless and her own person always neat.

The sea had called to Iain Macready from an early age. It was in his blood. His grandfather Macready—the descendant of an Irish emigrant in the potato famine of the eighteen-forties—had been drowned serving in the Navy in the Great War. It was in the air young Iain breathed, the ships coming and going an ingrained part of his boyhood. There was no other life for him but the sea.

At sixteen, he had signed on as cabin-boy and sailed away from the very docks he had haunted almost from the time he could walk. His grandmother had watched him go, her face giving no sign of her inner feelings. She was a woman who never outwardly showed emotion. If she had ever shed tears, it had been done in private.

Throughout the early months of the Second World War, the time which afterwards became known as the 'phoney war'—commercial shipping companies attempted to carry on their trading as normally as possible. Young Macready, mostly at sea, scarcely realised his country was supposed to be at war.

On Monday, the eighth of April, 1940, the ship in which Macready had signed on as cabin-boy out of Leith a few days earlier docked in a small port on the western coast of Denmark and began to offload its cargo. Captain Sinclair spent much of that first day ashore making arrangements to take on a cargo the following day. That evening, when he returned to his ship, everything seemed as usual, as it always had been whenever they had been moored in this harbour...

At dawn on the following morning, the Germans launched an offensive against neutral Denmark and Norway. By the afternoon, the whole of Denmark had been overrun and the Danish Government had capitulated to the Germans. The British sailors, caught unawares by the suddenness of the attack, watched helplessly as, at gunpoint, the German soldiers confiscated all the navigational instruments from their ship and threatened the seamen with internment for the duration of the war.

Captain Telfer Sinclair, a dour Scot with a thick Glaswegian accent, cursed and stormed and kept his men on board the ship marooned in the harbour, virtual prisoners of the Germans. Nightly the Scottish sailors hung over their ship's rail, ridiculing the Nazi soldiers who strutted up and down the harbour wall on duty. Goaded by the tone of their voices more than by actually being able to understand the words, the sentries would level their guns towards the boat, the sailors would duck down and a volley of gunshot would fly warningly over their heads. As the echoes died away into the night air the Scots would sing out, 'Missed again, Fritzie!'

The Captain would watch his crew's antics from his bridge, making no effort to curb this nightly horseplay, half wishing he could join in.

Macready, only half aware of the seriousness of their position, joined in with youthful enthusiasm. Only when one shot narrowly missed his head and ricochetted off the ship's superstructure behind him, did he realise that this was no game.

With thoughtful eyes, Captain Sinclair watched one of the harbour's tugs chugging up and down. This particular tug was operated by an old friend of his. Once they had both been captains of ships and their paths had crossed again and again during their life at sea. Then Captain Niels Andersen had been injured in a bad storm which had sunk his ship and taken the lives of three of his crew. He had retired from a life on the open sea but had since been employed on the tugs in his home port.

In a dark, sheltered corner of the harbour Captain Sinclair waited for his old friend. He watched the tug ease itself into place to nestle beside the harbour wall. A few minutes later he saw Andersen leave the vessel, hunch his shoulders against the driving rain lashing along the quay and begin to walk away.

Captain Sinclair whistled softly and Andersen hesitated, turned and peered into the shadows.

'Niels, my old friend,' Captain Sinclair called softly. 'Can ye spare a moment?'

Andersen walked slowly towards the voice, still hesitant, still uncertain who had called his name. He drew closer and then relief was in his tone as he said, 'Ah, it is you, Telfer Sinclair. But I am so sorry to see you still here.'

The two men shook hands warmly and withdrew once more into the black, concealing shadows.

'Niels—will you help us to get away?'

'Ah, my old friend,' the Dane said dazedly. 'I still cannot understand what has happened—or how. We have been hearing such dreadful tales. I would help you—you know that—but I have a wife and family and...'

'I know, I know. I wouldna ask you to be involved. We would arrange it at a time when you are on leave, say, or...'

'Then what is it you want of me?'

'I want to borrow your tug.'

Andersen laughed softly in the darkness. 'She is yours, my friend. Tomorrow I begin three days' leave. No one will touch her whilst I am away. There is no need now. Scarcely any ships coming or going, eh?' He shrugged hopelessly and then, even amidst all the trouble, he managed to raise a chuckle as he added, 'Except yours, my brave Captain.'

'Will the soldiers suspect anything?'

Andersen raised his shoulders. 'They have not interfered with me since they came. We will hope not.'

They shook hands once more. 'Good luck, my friend, good luck,' Andersen murmured and moved away through the rain.

That was the last time Captain Sinclair ever saw his Danish friend.

Captain Sinclair watched and waited his chance. Close to the harbour was a tavern frequented by sailors and now by the Nazi soldiers too. The British sailors, frustrated by the confines of their ship when such pleasures lay only yards away, embarked upon a campaign to visit the establishment. Their Captain actively encouraged the scheme and told them of his own plan.

They chose a dark, wet night when no moonlight penetrated the thick cloud, when the sea was a black, concealing, moving being and the dockside was a cold, rain-drenched inhospitable place. The Nazi sentry was huddled in a doorway when the sailors crept down the gangway in ones and twos and slipped through the shadows towards the fuzzy lights of the tavern. Once inside they mingled freely with the off-duty enemy soldiers, pretending to drink vast quantities of alcohol and giving oscar-winning performances of aimiability towards their captors.

'Ach, you're a grand laddie, Frishzie, to tek all we've been giving ye these last days.'

The Germans smiled and raised their mugs and nodded expansively toward their captives for the war was going well for Germany. They were sure of victory and could afford to be generous to the vanquished, to these poor Britishers who in a few days would be transported to camps in Germany. If they ever returned to their Britain, it would be to a very different place, Fritzie believed, under the rule of the Third Reich. The Germans watched their British prisoners enjoying their last moments of comparative freedom and apparently growing steadily drunker by the hour.

Eventually the sailors bade an excessively fond farewell to the German soldiers with much back-slapping and camaraderie. They staggered from the tavern and lurched along the dockside shouting and singing raucously, '...On the Bonnie, Bonnie Banks of Loch Lo-o-omond.' They gathered in an unsteady semi-circle around the lone sentry in his sheltered doorway.

From behind them came the soft 'phut-phut-phut' of the tug chugging up and down the harbour. Only the British sailors knew that instead of Captain

Niels Andersen, their own First Mate was operating the tug.

On board their ship, Captain Sinclair strained to see through the rain and the darkness and then whispered to young Macready at his side, 'Right, laddie, away now.'

The boy, who had stayed on board with his Captain, slipped down the gangway, obscured from the German sentry by his rollicking shipmates. He ran, soft-footed, towards the forward mooring-post and unhooked the two hawsers. Lying flat on his stomach at the edge of the quay and feeling his arms almost pulled from their sockets by the heavy ropes, he hung over the black water. Waiting his moment until the roistering sailors' voices rose higher and higher he let slip the hawsers into the water. Then he scrambled up and, half-crouching, scurried to do the same with the aft mooring ropes, then back to the gangway and up it on to the deck where he crouched down, panting heavily.

'Well done, laddie, well done!' were his Captain's whispered words of praise.

Captain Sinclair stood up and gave a shrill whistle. At once the drunken sailors closed in upon the German. A knife flashed and was sunk into the enemy's ribs and he fell back against the door, slithering to the ground. The sailors backed away still shouting, still calling 'goodnight' to the now dead sentry and gave every appearance of returning reluctantly to their ship under the stern eye of their Captain who waited at the top of the gangway.

As the last man stepped on to the deck, the gangway was hauled aboard. Then the little tug moved forward and gently nosed the big ship away from the quay side. A cable was thrown down and slowly the British ship was towed towards the harbour entrance. Far below, the engineer waited for the signal to start the ship's own engines.

They were almost out into the open sea when the alarm was given and the dockside became alive with scurrying figures. At once Captain Sinclair gave orders for the engines to be started. The tug disconnected and drew alongside. The First Mate scrambled up the rope ladder back on to his own ship leaving the tug drifting in the harbour waters.

As the ship's own engines took over, Captain Sinclair heard the gunshot from the quay but they were just out of range, the bullets plopping harmlessly into the escaping ship's wake.

'Be God, we've done it!' the Captain muttered as they forged ahead into the open sea. 'We've got awa' frae the bastards!'

He allowed his men a few moments of madness, drunk now, not from liquor but with heady success. But then the serious business of getting themselves home began. They had set out with neither charts, nor compass nor any such navigational aid, without even binoculars or a telescope. As best he could, Captain Sinclair steered their course north-westwards by the stars, partially obscured though they were by scudding clouds.

At last they sighted land, not knowing if they approached friend or enemy. They anchored off-shore and hoisted a distress signal and watched as a small boat put to sea from the flat shoreline and headed towards them.

Macready's sharp young eyes identified the orange and blue and white craft first. 'It's the lifeboat!' We're hame.'

Indeed they were home—but not to Scotland. They were much further south than their home port. They had anchored off the flat Lincolnshire coastline near the town of Saltershaven. All but the Captain, who would not leave his ship, were taken ashore and made welcome by the people of the coastal town.

Young Macready found himself at the home of the lifeboat coxswain, fussed over and cosseted by the coxswain's wife and shy daughter, Mary, who was a few years younger than Iain.

The next day the crew returned to their ship which was then guided into Grimsby dock where it awaited refitting of the instruments confiscated by the Germans. The sailors travelled home to Scotland to find other ships or to enlist now that they had realised just what this war was going to mean. The 'phoney war' for these men was over—they had seen for themselves the need to defend their homeland.

Iain Macready humped his knapsack towards the terrace house he called home to tell his grandmother that he had already enlisted in the Royal Navy. She took his news and listened to the tale he had to tell with interest but without showing any emotion. Only as the tall young man whom she had raised, his slight frame already filling out, his shoulders broadening, his long easy stride showing his growing self-confidence—only as he walked away from her with a cheery wave did Grandmother Macready allow her old eyes to fill with tears.

It was the last time he was to see the woman who had been everything in his life for on his first leave from the Navy he returned to Clydeside to find the streets around the dock flattened, the houses a smouldering pile of rubble.

In March 1941, Hitler's bombs, aiming for the docks, had wiped away Macready's home and his only close relative in one night. Iain Macready slung his knapsack over his shoulder and turned his back on his boyhood.

The sea was now his home.

But on one lonely leave, Macready, now a strong rugged twenty-year-old, went back to Saltershaven to visit the people who had shown him such kindness. Hearing of his orphaned state, the coxswain and his wife would hear of nothing else but that he should spend all his leaves with them. Iain Macready became involved with the lifeboat, becoming a willing crew member when Coxswain Randall found himself short of a hand. After the war, because there was no reason to return to Scotland, Saltershaven became his home. He married Mary Randall and when her father retired from active service on the lifeboat, Macready left the Royal Navy, but not the sea for he became the Saltershaven lifeboat's first full-time Coxswain/mechanic.

Mary had been an ideal wife for a seaman. She was shy and reserved but bred to the ways of the sea and possessed a quiet courage. Their life together had been a good one and Macready still missed her acutely for she had died of cancer after twenty-five years of marriage.

Now at fifty-eight, Macready was within two years of his own retirement from the lifeboat service, but for the moment the sea and the lifeboat—and his daughter—were his life.

The sea had always been Macready's life. He loved it, respected it, was exhilarated by it but, strangely, he had rarely been afraid of it. His trust in it had never been tested.

Macready could not believe that the sea that he loved so much could ever betray him.

CHAPTER 4

The Milner boys were enjoying their game of pretence. Backwards and forwards they had pushed the dinghy, jumping in and out of it, falling into the surf but laughing at the soaking, their tee-shirts soon wet and clinging.

'Now, come on, our Martin, I'm coxswain.' Nigel pursed his lips and tried to whistle like he had heard Macready at the launch.

'Aw, Nigel, you've bin coxswain all the time. It's my turn now.'

'No, it ain't. You're head launcher—and crew,' he added as an afterthought.

' 'Tain't fair,' Martin grumbled but knew if he wanted to continue playing he would have to give way as always to his elder brother.

'We've got a long trip this time. There's a fishin'-boat struck an iceberg.' Nigel was at least imaginative if highly inaccurate, and Martin did as he was told.

'Full ahead,' Nigel shouted, facing out

to sea, and made a guttural, engine-like noise in his throat.

'What am I supposed to do?' Martin asked.

'You be the radio man. Call up—call up somebody and tell 'em.'

'Tell 'em what?'

'Where we're goin' 'n that. Then you come and tell me what they say an' I say "Roger".'

'Right.' Martin twiddled imaginary knobs and spoke into his invisible radio/mike. 'Hello, hello, lifeboat calling beach. We're going to rescue a fishing-boat that's struck an iceberg. Yes—yes.' He turned to Nigel. 'He says...'

The engine noise stopped momentarily. 'You salute me and call me "Coxswain" or "sir". Brrrm, brrrm.' The engine noise began again.

'Coxswain, he says it's about five miles out to sea.'

'Give me a direction.'

'Eh?'

'A direction, stupid! You know, say "north by northwest", or something.'

'Oh.' Martin gaped around him as if expecting the sea to give him inspiration, a compass to appear out of the sky. He glanced to right and left and then behind him. Then slowly he turned right round and faced the beach—at least where the beach ought to be.

'Nigel!'

'Brrrm—*Coxswain*—brrrm, brrrm.'

'Nigel—where's t'beach? I can't see the beach.'

'Wha...?' All noise, save the sound of the sea, stopped and Martin felt the dinghy rock as Nigel turned round, felt the older boy's body close to him.

They crouched, one behind the other, gaping towards the shore squinting through the swirling mist.

Nigel's mouth dropped open, his eyes widened. Panic surged up into his chest, gripping his throat. He couldn't speak, couldn't move except to reach out towards Martin and grip the young boy's arm and stare helplessly, at the mist all around them enclosing them in a circle of seawater.

In the top flat, Joe Milner, step-father of the two boys, snorted in his sleep and then, as if the sound had disturbed him, he opened his eyes. He yawned noisily, stretched and glanced at his wife lying beside him. She was on her back, her open

57

mouth without its false teeth shrunken and falling inwards, making her look older than her thirty-seven years. Her black hair, frizzed with frequent perming, was already liberally speckled with grey. Her face had become tanned this last week, whilst he, with fairer colouring, had burnt and blistered, a layer of skin peeling like tissue paper from his shoulders. Gingerly he touched his nose which was still sore. He heaved himself out of bed and hitched up his pyjama trousers. He wore no jacket, only a vest. He had reached the end of the bed on his way to the bathroom down the landing, when the dull thud in his head and a funny weakness in his legs reminded him of the gallon and a half of bitter he had drunk the previous night. He belched loudly and fell across the end of the bed landing heavily on his wife's feet.

Blanche—had there ever been anyone so misnamed?—woke up swearing. 'What the bloody 'ell...? Ugh—I might 'ave known!' She drew her knees up out of his way and turned herself on to her side. 'Noisy bugger!' she whistled through her flabby mouth and closed her eyes again.

It wasn't until twenty past eleven that

they first missed the boys, but even then they knew of no reason to worry. Every morning of the holiday the boys had played quite safely on the beach until their parents had surfaced around eleven or later.

So why should this morning—the last day of their holiday—be any different?

Bleary-eyed and wobbly, Blanche Milner began to stuff her clothes into a suitcase. Breakfast was a cigarette and a cup of instant coffee—if Joe could be nagged into putting the kettle on.

'Where's them little buggers got to? Don't they know the train goes at one?'

Joe sniffed and coughed juicily. 'They'll be on t'beach.'

' *Course* they'll be on t'beach. I know that,' she shrilled scornfully. 'But I wants 'em 'ere packing, not playin', not this morning. Go'n look for 'em, Joe.'

He made a token resistance, not moving until she shrieked warningly, *Joe,* you hear me?'

He flopped down the three flights of stairs and out of the rear entrance into the back yard. Four cars belonging to other occupants of the flats had been squeezed into the square. To the left, against a brick wall was a sort of lean-to where beach gear—deck-chairs, buckets and spades, balls and various objects—could be left instead of being carted all the way up the stairs to the flats.

Joe Milner stopped. In the middle of all the clutter was an open space where their dinghy should have been. But the black and orange inflatable was not there.

'The little...!' he began, but strangely he was not given to swearing as frequently and volubly as his wife, and he contented himself with planning the various punishments he would inflict upon the disobedient boys when he caught up with them.

He shambled through the alley dividing their block of holiday flats from the next in the row which ran the full length of the Marine Esplanade overlooking the foreshore gardens, the putting-greens, the bowling-greens and the boating-lake, and beyond them the wide expanse of beach and the sea. Joe walked along the esplanade, past the lifeboat station with its doors still wide open, the empty trailer and tractor standing at the ready for the recall to the beach. Skirting the fountain he walked down Beach Road and on to the sand.

Visibility was clearer now. A light off-shore breeze had blown away the last vestiges of the early-morning mist and the sands were dotted with people, families entrenching themselves for the day. But on Saturdays, change-over day, the beach was understandably less crowded than on any other day of the week.

Joe's tired eyes watered against the brightness as he scanned the sands and the water's edge. He spotted two minute figures cavorting in the shallows and he began to struggle across the soft sand towards them. Beads of sweat sprang out on his forehead and prickled his armpits and his calf muscles began to ache. The tide was about halfway between high and low water now and Joe had to wade through a creek to reach the sea itself.

'Little sods!' he muttered. 'I won't 'alf give 'em what for when I catches up wi' 'em!'

About fifty yards from the children, he stopped, blinked and rubbed his eyes. He could see now that the two children were not his stepsons. One was a boy of a similar age, but the other was a little girl, dressed in a frilled bathing-suit. Unaware of the man standing watching them, the two children continued digging the trench, squealing with delight as the waves ran up their channel and around the moat of their sandcastle.

Joe Milner glanced to right and left along the beach.

Then where the hell were Nigel and Martin?

The first moments of panic had passed and Nigel released his brother's arm.

'Come on,' he said roughly, as if to rouse not only Martin but himself too from their petrified state. 'It can't be that far away. We can paddle back.'

But the younger boy still shivered and shook. His teeth rattled with fear and now with cold for the breeze was growing stronger with every minute. 'But where—which w-way?' he whimpered. 'We don't know which—way to g-go.'

For a moment Nigel hesitated, confused, then he said scornfully, 'It's the way the waves are going, stupid! Where's them paddles?'

Martin, still shaking as if with the ague,

hadn't moved. 'Paddles? I don't know.'

'Didn't you bring them?'

Martin's eyes widened as he shook his head numbly. 'You stupid little bugger...' Nigel screeched, sounding so much like their mother that Martin cowered beneath the expected blow.

'Now we'll have to use our hands to paddle,' Nigel ordered. 'Come on, get crackin'.'

Martin dabbled his hand ineffectually in the water, whilst Nigel leaned over the edge and made sweeping movements deep into the water. The dinghy began to move, not forwards but round and round in a spin.

Nigel stopped and lashed out at his brother. 'Idiot! You'll have to do it harder than that. We'll just go round in circles else.'

Martin began to whimper and shiver. His tee-shirt and shorts were wet through and the further they drifted out to sea the colder it seemed to get.

'Eh, wait a minute, I reckon I saw summat then,' Nigel shouted. 'Yeh—look, the beach, I can see t'beach.'

The mist was being blown away by the strengthening breeze, but it did not bring consolation to the two boys.

Forlornly—they stared towards the shore. Martin hiccuped, the tears flowing now unchecked.

'It's so far away—it looks miles.'

'Don't be daft!' Nigel tried to say, but his words lacked conviction even to himself and as Martin added hopelessly, 'We can't paddle it that far. We can't get back. We can't never get back!' for once the older boy was silent.

In fact the inflatable was only a few hundred yards from the shore but it might as well have been the miles it seemed to the two boys for all the chance they had of getting themselves back. Still no one saw them. The lifeboat was heading south in the opposite direction to that in which the boys were being carried, and the coastguard's landrover was speeding along the coast road towards the marshes of Dolan's Sand.

Across the saltmarsh south of Dolan's Point, behind a grass-covered sandbank two figures lay prone, their elbows resting on the ground, a pair of field-glasses to their eyes.

'See it, Mel?'

'Yep. It's the lifeboat all right,' the girl answered.

'See? I told yer we could fetch it out wiv them flares we found.'

The girl giggled. 'Look at 'em swannin' up an' down there. An' they don't even know what they're looking for.'

'They don't know they're looking for nothing!' the boy said and his girlfriend rolled over on to her back shaking with laughter.

The boy lowered the binoculars. 'Eh Mel, where do you reckon we could get hold of some more of them flare things?'

Her fit of the giggles subsided. She sat up and wiped the tears from her eyes. 'I dunno. Do they sell 'em round here?'

'Hey—I arn't buyin' 'em!' the boy said indignantly. 'That ain't my scene.'

'Nick 'em then.'

'Yea, but where from?'

Thoughtfully the pair gazed across the marsh at the boat ploughing up and down the stretch of water.

Macready turned the lifeboat at the end of another run and then throttled back to dead slow. His crew relaxed their vigil and congregated in the coxswain's cockpit.

'Nothing,' was the agreed opinion.

'Pete?' The coxswain looked towards his R/T operator.

Pete Donaldson turned, his eyes slightly red-rimmed from concentrated staring at the radar screen. 'Nope—nothing here either.'

'Hmph,' Macready grunted, his eyes scanning the gently swelling ocean. As if in answer to his moment of indecision, the radio receiver crackled and the coastguard call-sign from his landrover came over the air.

Pete replied that their search had so far proved futile. During the two and a quarter hours since they had arrived at the area given, the lifeboat had cruised the St Botolphs Deeps, had passed through Freeman Channel further out into the Wash and had then headed north-eastwards again along the eastern edge of the sandbank known as Long Sand. North of that lay another, smaller, bank, the Inner Dog's Head and it was off the eastern edge of this that the lifeboat now cruised when at ten minutes past mid-day Jack Hansard's next message came across the airwaves. '...I'm still at the Point. I've walked across Dolan's Sands and on to the Haven Flats and I can't see anything here either now. I've also just had a report from the police about two missing boys. Their father thinks they've got an inflatable dinghy with them. We're not sure they're even in the sea, but it's a possibility. Over.'

The men standing in the coxswain's cockpit exchanged a look—a look that said it all.

Macready put out his hand for the radio/telephone and spoke directly to Jack Hansard. 'Saltershaven mobile, this is Saltershaven lifeboat. Coxswain speaking. How long have the boys been missing? Over.'

'...They don't know. The father says they must have gone off before they—the parents—woke up. You know the sort of thing?'

'Aye,' Macready muttered shortly, more to himself than to the coastguard. He knew only too well how a happy holiday could so easily end in tragedy because of indolent parents.

The coastguard was speaking again. 'I'm on my way back to the station now.

There's nothing more I can do here. Out.'

Without Jack Hansard needing to go into detail over the radio, Macready knew the coastguard's landrover would be heading back either for the coastguard's station on the seafront or possibly to the lifeboat station. There he would obtain further information from the police, or the boys' father, and then he would consult the lifeboat secretary and call up Macready again.

'Well, while we're waiting,' the coxswain said, 'we might as well carry on a while here.'

Once more the crew returned to their posts and the *Mary Martha Clamp* headed towards the Outer Dog's Head sandbank, Macready keeping to a northerly course just in case they were needed to search for the boys.

Half an hour later, Bill Luthwaite's voice came over the radio link from the coastguard's vehicle. '...The Inshore Lifeboat has launched to search for these boys. We think you should stay where you are at present and let the ILB do a search first. Over.'

Macready agreed and then asked, 'Is the

helicopter on stand-by?'

An air/sea rescue helicopter operated from an R.A.F base in Norfolk and often assisted in a search and rescue operation in Macready's area. Bill Luthwaite replied that it was but that they would only request assistance if the inshore boat failed to find the boys fairly quickly.

Macready gave a grunt of satisfaction and was about to hand over the telephone to Pete Donaldson once more when another thought struck him. '...Jack, get on to the boathouse and see if any of our lads noticed any boys watching our launch this morning.'

The coastguard's voice now came noisily into the cockpit of the lifeboat. '...Right, it's a possibility. Out.'

Macready now handed the phone back to Pete, who, ten minutes later was relaying another message from the coastguard to his coxswain. 'Jack says Tim Matthews saw two lads amongst the watchers at the launch. Tim reckons they didn't seem that interested though. They scampered off before the lifeboat was out of sight.'

Macready smiled at the thought of Tim's indignation at such an action. But Jack's next words, relayed by Pete, replaced

Macready's amusement with intuitive fore-boding. 'Tim's rough description of those lads fits the missing boys though.'

'Mmm, well, if it was them, that helps a bit as regards time.' Once more Macready reached out to take the radio/telephone to speak directly to the coastguard and the lifeboat secretary.

'Saltershaven coastguard, this is Salters-haven lifeboat. Coxswain speaking. I suppose we could make a pretty fair guess at the time they could have entered the water—say half an hour after our launch?'

Jack Hansard agreed and added, 'The holiday flats they're staying in are pretty near the lifeboat station, so I'd say they'd go in off-central beach. If it was them watching your launch, it could even be the same place the lifeboat entered the water.'

Macready made swift calculations in his head. He had no need to look at his charts, not just to make a rough estimate as to where the boys' dinghy might be, he knew the area so well.

'... That could put the dinghy out of the inshore boat's range by now. Over.'

'Affirmative. Suggest you make for the

area right away, but we'll let the inshore boat carry on the search until you get up here again. Over.'

'And the helicopter?' Macready wanted to know.

'We'll ask Breymouth to request assistance.'

'Right,' Macready said decisively. 'We're on our way. Roger and out.'

Now the boys could not even see the beach for they were huddled in the bottom of the dinghy cold, wet and very frightened. Martin's tears had subsided to the occasional sniffle but he was shivering uncontrollably. The inflatable drifted north-eastwards at the rate of approximately three knots carried by the ebbing tide and pushed further by the south-westerly offshore breeze. The sea seemed, to the boys, much rougher out here. The little black-and-orange dinghy tossed and bucked and the waves slapped against the sides, splashing water over the edge and drenching the already bedraggled pair.

'Nigel,' Martin whimpered. 'I feel sick.'

'Well, 'ang yer 'ead over the side. I don't want it all over me!' snapped the

71

unsympathetic fat boy. He was uncomfort-
ably wet and the cold was just beginning
to penetrate even his extra layers of fat,
but nausea—even out here on the rolling
ocean—never worried Nigel.

'Eh, I've just thought.' Excitement, hope
was in Nigel's voice. 'The lifeboat! It'll see
us when it comes back.'

He was struggling to stand up, raising his
arms, already convinced that the lifeboat
would see him at once. 'But we ought to
wave...'

The dinghy rocked dangerously.

'Oooh, Nigel, don't. You'll tip us over!'
Martin screeched but at that second the
fat boy slipped on the wet plastic and
fell on to one side of the dinghy, his
weight squashing the inflated side. Martin,
weak with cold and sea-sickness, slithered
helplessly towards Nigel, landing in a
sprawling heap against him. The dinghy
tipped up, the lighter side leaving the
water, and the side where the two boys
were dipping almost beneath the waves.
Martin was wedged in the corner of the
dinghy but Nigel, already half over the
side, slipped backwards.

There was nothing to save him on the
slippery PVC—his head and shoulders

dipped beneath the water, his arms threshed and his legs flailed the air.

Martin watched in horror as, almost in slow motion, Nigel slid into the sea.

CHAPTER 5

Mike Harland had discovered gliding four years ago. He had come upon it by accident. Out cycling around the Lincolnshire Wolds one summer Sunday about four miles from the village where he lived, he had been startled by the sudden appearance of a glider surging up from behind a clump of trees. Intrigued, he had pedalled towards it. Closer he could see the cable pulling the glider higher and higher, climbing into the sky at an angle of about forty-five degrees.

But how? And where?

The how was a winch attached to the end of a converted double-decker bus and the where was a disused Lincolnshire airfield which the glider club had rescued and resuscitated. Instead of the Lancaster bombers blundering down the runways and lifting reluctantly into the air, now the silent, ethereal bird-like craft skimmed smoothly across the grass and soared upwards into the sky.

Mike Harland had leant across his handlebars and stared, open-mouthed and fascinated.

He was back the following weekend determined to get a flight. He signed a form to become a day member of the Golden Eagle Gliding Club, paid his flight fee and the launch fee and went up for two separate flights of ten minutes duration with one of the club's instructors.

That was just the beginning.

Mike was twenty-three and in the final stages of becoming a qualified architect. He was not particularly tall, thin and with floppy straight mouse-coloured hair and hazel eyes, and a mouth that was a little inclined to sulkiness. It happened that he was between girlfriends at the moment when gliding entered his life and took it over.

Like all the converted, he became more fanatical about it than the original devotees. It was an expensive hobby. Sometimes he didn't eat lunch mid-week to be sure of getting a flight at the weekend, though he was careful to keep this fact hidden from his widowed mother with whom he still lived. Girlfriends of the past faded into obscurity. The only girls he even noticed were the one or two at the gliding club.

He took a course of instruction, passed all the tests, put in all the necessary flying hours and flew solo.

It was like being transported from the mundane world into a heavenly existence. Not content with just bumming around the sky above the airfield, Mike Harland became addicted to gaining as many of the awards for gliding as he could. Whilst it was necessary for him to do distance and duration flying to obtain each stage, nevertheless it was cloud flying that intrigued and exhilarated him. Whilst his club-mates flew ever-increasing distances across country, Mike's one aim was to climb higher and higher, ever higher.

And on this particular Bank Holiday weekend he had the chance—if the weather conditions were only right—to try for his first diamond badge—an in-flight height gain of five thousand metres.

At the moment when the maroons were being fired on that Saturday morning, twenty miles to the north west of Salters-haven and five miles due west inland from the coast, Mike Harland was listening to a weather report over the telephone.

The general weather forecast broadcast on the radio earlier had said *'...all areas dry, very warm and mainly sunny, although the sunshine may be rather hazy at times. Maximum temperatures twenty-six centigrade (seventy-nine Fahrenheit). Winds light, south-westerly...'*

But Mike needed a more detailed forecast and one specifically for flying conditions. So he phoned the regional meteorological office, who reported that there was likely to be very little or no cloud that day and consequently the freezing level would be very high, approximately ten thousand feet. The south-westerly winds would be light and variable.

It was a disappointing forecast for Mike for without the lift provided by the thermals to cloud base, it was unlikely he would be able to achieve the kind of height he needed. Still, perhaps if he could be one of the first off the ground he would have the whole day in front of him.

When Mike propped up his bike at the side of the airfield, he could see that one or two members of the gliding club were already there bringing out the gliders from the hanger. The landrover towed the office, a blue-painted caravan affectionately known as 'the box', to the north-east corner of the field from where they would be launching today into the wind.

In one end of the caravan, positioned today to face to the south-west, were two huge lights, like searchlights, which were flashed to give signals to the winchman. Across the field, almost three quarters of a mile away, were the two buses, a double-decker and a single-decker. These had been converted to run a winch each. On each winch were two drums with a cable on each one, making four cables in all. A tractor with a frontal bar and hooks took the four cables at once across the field to the launching area and dropped them in a square marked with bollards and then returned to the buses to repeat the operation when all four winch cables had been used.

Mike joined in bringing the ready-rigged gliders out and across the grass to the east side of the field to wait in line for each launch. Several more members began to arrive, some with their own gliders packed in thirty-foot trailers behind their cars. These would need to be rigged by at least three people. Each member of the club took his turn in helping with the ground jobs connected with launching, recording, signalling and so on, and helped rig and de-rig the various sailplanes.

Mike approached the duty pilot of the day, Dave Armstrong. 'Any chance of me being first away today, Dave? I'd like a shot at my diamond height.'

'Ah, Mike. Sorry, but I've had to put you down for winch duty today. Chris was down to do it, but his wife rang me this morning. He's got one of these summer flu virus things. In a hell of a state, he is.'

Mike pulled a face. 'I was hoping to get away early. There'll not be much lift today anyway and...'

'Look, just do it for the first hour, will you? I'll get someone to take over from you at eleven and I'll put you down for launch at eleven-thirty. Okay?'

There was no arguing with Dave Armstrong, so Mike nodded reluctantly and went to the office to book his flight time. Every flight had to be recorded and each award attempt declared before take-off, and logs completed.

'Can I book the Blanik for an eleven-thirty launch, Toby? And can I borrow your barograph, mate? I want to have a shot at diamond height today.'

'You can borrow the barograph, Mike, but I'm afraid the Blanik's booked. Harry's instructing in it today.'

'Oh damn!' Mike muttered. 'What is available then?'

Toby Wingate consulted his list. 'The ASK 13 is the only twin-seater available. There are two single-seaters—the K6 and the Pirat.'

Mike gave a click of annoyance. 'I don't like any of them. They don't handle like the Blanik. Oh well, book me down for the ASK 13.'

'Right.' Toby wrote the details on his list. He looked up at Mike again and asked tentatively, 'I don't suppose you'd take a visitor up first, would you?' He nodded towards the window of the caravan. 'That girl out there wants two flights. She's paid her day membership fee and flight fee.'

'Well, I can't do both,' Mike snapped. 'Have a go at the diamond *and* take someone up who's likely to throw up all over me and want to come down after ten minutes, can I? Besides, Dave's put me on

79

winch duty till eleven.'

'Aw, come on, Mike, don't be like that.' Toby Wingate was one of those placid people who didn't seem to mind however much he was put upon by the others. It seemed, Mike thought, as if Toby spent most of his time doing the ground jobs. To Mike's idea, Toby Wingate was a fool to himself.

Mike remained silent.

Toby sighed. 'All right then, I'll ask one of the others.'

Mike stomped away across the field towards the buses.

For an hour Mike winched other flyers into the air, watching with envious eyes as they soared off into the sky. Anxiously he scanned the cloud formations trying to plan his flight. But the sky remained annoyingly blue without any building cumulus to be seen. Every ten minutes he glanced at his watch whilst the hands crawled towards eleven o'clock.

Agitatedly he kept a look out for someone coming to relieve him on the winch and at ten minutes past eleven he saw one of the club members sauntering across the field towards the buses.

'Come on, Dan,' Mike shouted, 'I've a

flight booked at eleven-thirty.'

Dan grinned, but did not quicken his pace, '*Awf'ly* sorry, old chap. What's all the hurry?'

'I was hoping to get a shot at the height for my first diamond.'

'Haw, haw, medal-hunting again, are we? All right, old boy, off you scoot.'

Scowling, Mike ran across the grass towards the ASK 13 waiting next in line. He couldn't take the ribbing some of the members liked to hand out. They could not understand why Mike constantly chased all the awards available, whilst he, in turn, could not understand their being content to drift aimlessly around the sky without achieving some goal.

Quickly he carried out the routine daily check and climbed in. One of the club members held the sailplane level and after completing the cockpit checks and attaching the cable, the necessary signals were given and Mike was away across the grass, bumping slightly for a few yards until, with the aid of the flaps, the glider lifted from the ground and soared upwards. For the first hundred feet Mike kept the angle of the climb gradual but then he gently steepened the climb to the optimum angle of about forty-five degrees.

At eight hundred feet there was a sudden snapping noise and the glider jerked dramatically. The airspeed indicator began to fall anti-clockwise, though the nose of the glider still pointed upwards.

'Blast!' Mike said aloud. 'A cable break! The last bloody thing I want now.'

Immediately he eased the stick forward so that the nose of the plane dropped to prevent the sailplane going into a stall. The airspeed indicator began to rise again and Mike eased the glider into a normal gliding position and began to calculate whether he had enough height to make a complete circuit and bring the plane down on the launching area again.

He operated the cable mechanism to release the portion of cable which would no doubt still be attached to the plane, though from his position in the cockpit he could not see how much remained. Deciding that he had insufficient height to be able to make the complete circuit to bring him back to the launch point, he turned towards that part of the field frequently used by the glider pilots when they failed to complete a normal circuit.

Here, the field was by no means as

smooth as the launching area and the glider bumped and clattered on landing, jolting Mike and almost making his teeth rattle. He brought the glider to a standstill only five feet from the hedge and for a moment he sat back in the cockpit and sighed with relief. Then the anger at being thwarted yet again in getting away early made him thump the control panel in a moment of sheer frustration.

Toby Wingate drove over in his car, jumping out and galloping towards him as Mike climbed out of the cockpit.

'Bloody cable break,' Mike greeted him shortly.

'You all right?' Toby panted.

' 'Course I'm all right, just bloody mad, that's all!'

'Let's tow her back then, shall we?'

'I suppose so,' Mike replied moodily, 'but I shan't get another launch in time today though, shall I?'

'Cheer up, mate,' Toby said cheerfully. 'There's tomorrow—and Monday. That's the best thing about a Bank Holiday weekend, at least we've got an extra day's flying.'

'Yes, I suppose you're right,' Mike agreed grudgingly. 'And damned if I'll be fobbed off tomorrow. Tomorrow I'm *first* away!'

'It's all your bloody fault,' Blanche Milner screeched, her fists pummelling her husband's shoulder. 'You should 'ave let the dinghy down.'

'It was you! Couldn't wait to get to your blasted bingo, could you?' Joe retorted.

Blanche's voice rose higher. 'You don't care about 'em—just 'cos they're not yourn!'

Appalled they stared at each other before Joe lumbered out of the room, leaving Blanche to throw herself across the bed and beat the pillow with her fists, screaming with rage and fear.

Downstairs the owner of the flats met Joe. Behind her, in their best coats and carrying heavy suitcases, stood a newly-arrived family of four—mother, father and two little girls.

'Mr Milner—you're supposed to be out of the flat by twelve noon. It is now...'

Joe ignored her, squeezing himself past the family.

'*Mr Milner...*'

'Look, missus,' he turned to face her, fear making him vent his anger on someone,

84

anyone. 'Us two lads is missin'. Us can't leave yet.'

'Well, really...' began the woman, but Joe was gone, leaving them all staring after him, the landlady open-mouthed, the family weighed down by their luggage.

Joe walked the short distance to the lifeboat station.

He was angry and frustrated. Angry with the two boys, fed up with his wife's nagging and reluctantly angry with himself for not having deflated the dinghy the previous night. Every other night of the holiday he had let the wretched thing down only to have to blow it up again the following morning. Then last night—their last complete day—the weather had been so warm that they had lingered on the beach until the last possible moment. Only Blanche with her bingo fever had at last nagged them into returning to the flats. Only her ill-temper that they would be late for the bingo session had caused him to leave the dinghy as it was.

Hesitantly now he approached the lifeboat station and hovered uncertainly in the open doorway. He cleared his throat and the young fellow coiling a rope and stowing it neatly in the small trailer looked up.

'Any—any news?' Joe asked.

Tim Matthews's expression was blank for a moment, then he realised. 'Oh sorry, sir, you're the boys' father?'

Joe nodded, relaxing a little. The lad seemed friendly, not blaming him as everyone else seemed to be doing. Even the policeman to whom Joe had first reported the fact that his two boys were missing, whilst being swiftly efficient, had seemed a little brusque with him as if it were his fault the lads had gone off like they had.

'I'm sorry, sir,' Tim was saying. 'No word yet. The inshore boat will be on its way back soon. But the offshore boat—' he indicated the huge empty carriage behind him—'has gone in search of your lads now, and the air/sea rescue helicopter will be called in. They'll soon find them, sir, don't you worry.'

But at one o'clock there was still no word of the missing boys and the train to Worksop left Saltershaven without the Milner family.

That was the worst thing about a Bank Holiday weekend, Macready thought as the lifeboat headed at full speed north-north-east on a bearing of 010 degrees

86

towards the area where he believed the inflatable might be, assuming that the two little boys were out on the ocean. Bank Holidays brought not only a run of genuine calls, but the hoax calls and the doubtful ones as well.

It said much for the patient character of the lifeboatman that even if he were unsure whether a search was really necessary or not, he still treated the service the same as any other. The only unanswerable question that such a doubtful report posed was—just how long should they go on searching?

At 13.40 the lifeboat reached the area Macready had ringed on his chart. The coxswain estimated that if the inflatable had begun to drift out to sea soon after their own launch, it would have been carried out by the ebbing tide and the offshore breeze at a rate of between three and four knots in a north-easterly direction. He planned to cover an area between 035 and 045 degrees working towards the north-east and his decision was backed by the headquarters at Breymouth.

The inshore boat, practically on the limit of its range, came alongside the larger boat. The inshore craft was this time crewed by reserves, because Phil Davis, Tony

Douglas and Pete Donaldson, any two of whom normally crewed the ILB, were already aboard the *Mary Martha Clamp*.

Macready spoke to Terry Lightfoot over the radio. 'We'll carry on the search from here, Terry.'

'Right, Mac. We'll put back now but continue to search on our way.'

Across the stretch of water the two men waved acknowledgement to each other.

The light offshore breeze had strengthened since morning to force three and the sun was bright in a cloudless blue sky, the sea a rippling, shimmering mirror.

In the bows Phil Davis screwed up his eyes against the glare whilst Pete Donaldson turned from his radio and looked up at his coxswain. 'Breymouth confirm the helicopter is on its way.'

Macready nodded as Pete added, 'I'm not likely to pick up a plastic dinghy on the radar, am I, Mac? Do you want me on deck?'

'Aye, another pair of eyes will help up here.'

As the ILB sped away back towards Saltershaven beach, Macready set a northerly course on a bearing of 350 degrees and eased the control forward to cruising speed. He kept on this course for two nautical miles and then turned eastwards for one mile and then abruptly south-south-easterly for four miles on a reciprocal bearing of 155 degrees to take him directly back across the estimated path of the drifting dinghy.

If—indeed—there was a drifting dinghy out here.

As he made this second turn, Pete Donaldson caught his eye and pointed towards the south. Macready looked and saw a tiny speck in the sky approaching rapidly. The Sea King helicopter. Pete then left the deck for a few minutes to call up the pilot of the Sea King.

'Rescue helicopter Five-five. Rescue helicopter Five-five, this is Saltershaven lifeboat, Saltershaven lifeboat. Do you read? Over.'

'Saltershaven lifeboat, Saltershaven lifeboat, this is Rescue Five-five. Rescue Five-five. Loud and clear. Go ahead. Over.'

Pete then gave the helicopter pilot details of the lifeboat's planned course and the pilot replied, 'Saltershaven lifeboat, this is Rescue Five-five. Message received and understood. We will fly further out and work back towards you. Out.'

Both Breymouth Coastal Rescue Head-quarters and Jack Hansard came on the air to confirm that they had heard the exchange of conversation between the lifeboat and the helicopter and now knew exactly what was happening out at sea.

The time was 14.10. For the next hour the *Mary Martha Clamp* continued on her box-like zigzag pattern of search whilst a few miles to the north-east the Sea King adopted a similar method, skimming only feet above the waves.

At 15.12 the helicopter pilot's voice came over the radio/telephone again and Pete hurried to respond.

'... We have sighted an object in the water fifty-three degrees seventeen minutes north, zero degrees thirty-six minutes east. Over.'

The lifeboat was three and a half nautical miles away and Macready immediately set a course for the position on the chart given by the pilot. Pete relayed his coxswain's message. '...Lifeboat heading on bearing zero-three-zero at full speed. Will be with you in about thirty minutes. Over.'

Now the crew shifted their positions towards the bows of the lifeboat, each man eager to be the first to spot the dinghy. Pete Donaldson now remained near his radio/telephone.

Twenty-three minutes after they had received the message from the air/sea rescue helicopter, Tony Douglas pointed and shouted excitedly, 'Mac—there's something over there.' All eyes now turned to look in the direction Tony pointed. The helicopter was circling above the area.

'There's summat there,' Fred muttered to himself and signalled his agreement. Macready swung the wheel and the boat turned a few degrees to starboard, heading for the bobbing black object that Tony's sharp eyes had spotted.

'I reckon it's them,' Tony shouted. 'Here, let's have those glasses, Dad.'

He trained the binoculars, squinting against the mercurial water. 'Yup, it's a dinghy right enough—an' I can see them in it—at least...'

He paused as the lifeboat sped closer.

Then slowly he lowered the glasses. Tony Douglas, father of two young children himself, turned towards his father, his face sombre.

'I can only see *one* bairn!'

CHAPTER 6

Julie Macready heard Howard's car as she was taking the casserole from the oven. She ran out to meet him.

'Hello there,' he called as he swung his legs from his car and bounded towards her, enveloping her in an enthusiastic bear-hug.

'Hello, Howard,' Julie said, a little shy of him, a little nervous of how he and her father would get along together.

The only other time the two men had met had been on Open Day at Julie's College, when her father had visited. Howard had joined them for the afternoon from the neighbouring University. There, Howard had been surrounded by his own kind, and it had been Macready who had felt out of place.

But this was Saltershaven.

Admittedly Howard was smartly dressed in a grey check suit and matching waistcoat, a yellow rose-bud in his lapel, but Julie hoped he had brought some less formal clothes for the weekend.

'Come and look what I've got.' Behind the car was a trailer and Howard was dragging her towards it. 'There, what do you say to that?'

Proudly he waved his arm to encompass the trailer and perched upon it a fifteen-foot sailing day-boat, with the name painted on the bows—*Nerissa.*

'Oh—a boat!' Julie said unnecessarily.

'Well, you might show a little more interest, old thing,' Howard said. 'Just the ticket, I thought, for a weekend by the sea.'

'Is—is it yours?'

'Oh yes,' Howard said airily. 'I bought her last week.'

'She's lovely—really lovely,' Julie said, but then she could not prevent the words from slipping out. 'But this coast is not terribly safe for sailing, you know. Not unless you really know what you're doing.'

'Know what I'm doing?' Howard laughed aloud. 'Of course I know what I'm doing. I'll have you know that some friends I used to spend all my hols with had a boat. We were hardly ever out of the thing.'

'Oh, that's all right then,' Julie said, relieved and added, 'Come along in and

I'll show you your room. Dad's out on a service, I'm afraid, and I've no idea when he'll be back. We won't wait dinn—I mean—lunch.' Dinner to Howard, she remembered, was at seven in the evening, not midday.

'A service? What is he—a parson or a motor mechanic?' Howard asked, laughing at his own joke.

'Neither. Didn't I tell you? He's the full-time coxswain/mechanic of our lifeboat.'

'Oh, rescues people who can't swim and kids in rubber dinghies, does he?' Howard guffawed again.

Ironically, she could make no retort for she now knew—Tim had rung through to tell her—that at this very moment her father was indeed searching an area of the ocean for two small boys in a dinghy.

As the *Mary Martha Clamp* drew alongside the black-and-orange inflatable, anxious faces peered over the side. Half-sitting, half-sprawling against the side of the dinghy was a semi-conscious Martin, his tee-shirt and shorts saturated, his arms and legs were white, almost a pale blue, from exposure. His eyes were swollen and his lips were cracked and parched by the salt water.

94

In the bottom of the dinghy lay the still figure of Nigel Milner.

Tony Douglas and Chas Blake clambered over the gunwales of the lifeboat and down the scramble net. Carefully, so as not to set it rocking, Tony stepped down into the dinghy and picked up the younger boy in his arms. Gently Tony handed him up to Chas, and Fred and Phil Davis hung over the side, reaching down with willing hands to help.

'Come on, me little laddo. You'll be all right now.'

At the sound of the voices of the rescuers, Martin opened his eyes and tried to speak. 'Me brother, what about me brother?' he whispered hoarsely.

'Dun't fret,' Fred reassured the shivering boy. 'We'll get him.'

'Mister—'ee fell over into the sea. I thought 'ee was drownded, but I got 'im back into the dinghy, but 'ee ain't moved since.'

Martin was borne away to the covered cockpit in the bows of the lifeboat.

Carefully, Tony squatted down beside the still figure in the dinghy. From at first having experienced a profound relief at seeing that the second boy was in the craft but out of sight until they were right up to it, Tony now felt a renewal of the fear and doubt wash over him. He felt for the boy's pulse. It was weak and fluttery—but there!

'He's alive,' he shouted jubilantly, 'but he's in worse shape than the other little lad.'

As Nigel was lifted into the lifeboat, Macready spoke to the pilot of the Sea King over the radio link and swiftly explained the situation. 'One boy's reasonably okay, but the other's in bad shape. He needs immediate hospital treatment.'

The pilot's voice came over loudly, 'Make ready to receive the winchman. Over.'

Macready acknowledged and handed the phone back to Pete. 'Keep in contact with him.'

Fred Douglas arrived in the coxswain's cockpit and took over the wheel, holding the lifeboat steady whilst Macready went for'ard to look at the boys. Squeezing his way beneath the protective tarpaulin covering the for'ard cockpit he glanced at one of the boys sitting huddled in blankets, but attacking a chocolate bar from the emergency rations on board.

Martin Milner was still suffering from shock, but Macready could see that he was in no danger now. He turned his attention to the motionless form on the stretcher being wrapped warmly by Tony and Phil.

'The pilot's all set to lower the winchman as soon as we're ready?' It was a question as well as a statement.

'About two minutes, Cox'n,' responded Tony Douglas, all the while his fingers deftly wrapping the boy in a warm blanket whilst Phil Davis was making sure the boy's nose and throat were clear and that he could breathe.

Macready returned aft to retake the wheel and relay the message through Pete to the helicopter pilot.

'Saltershaven lifeboat, this is Rescue Five-five. Suggest you steer course on bearing two-three-zero as we begin our approach. Over.'

Macready promptly turned the helm to bring the lifeboat pointing in the right direction.

'...Proceeding on course two-three-zero. Over,' Pete informed the pilot who at once began to manoeuvre his machine to hover about forty feet above the water astern of the lifeboat approaching at an angle of thirty degrees to the port side of the lifeboat so that the winchman and winch operator had the lifeboat in view all the time as he descended from the opening on the starboard side of the helicopter.

Macready watched as the winchman appeared and, swinging slightly, was lowered down towards them whilst Macready kept the lifeboat at a steady speed. The air was filled with noise, the draught from the whirling propellers flattening the waves around the lifeboat as the helicopter came nearer and nearer. The winchman landed on the flat surface of the box at the stern of the boat and immediately disconnected himself from the winch line. The helicopter swung away for a short distance until Nigel Milner had been strapped and secured to the Neil Robertson stretcher the winchman had brought down with him.

The signal was given that they were ready and Pete called up the helicopter which moved in again. The winchman caught the swinging cable and attached it to himself and the stretcher and then steadily they were hauled aloft, swaying and twisting round and round, towards the helicopter.

The faces of the lifeboat crew were upturned towards the Sea King still droning noisily above them, until they saw that the stretcher was safely aboard. The helicopter lifted and swung away towards the coast.

Within minutes the boy would be at a hospital.

Macready swung the wheel and turned the *Mary Martha Clamp* towards Salters-haven, pausing only whilst two members of his crew retrieved the inflatable from the water. Pete Donaldson was speaking on the R/T to Breymouth informing them that the boys had been found, the service completed and that the lifeboat was returning to Saltershaven, the estimated time of arrival being 17.45.

When the lifeboat beached, Joe and Blanche Milner were waiting on the sands with a policeman. So was Jack Hansard, who came right to the water's edge in his landrover to pick up the casualty. At the end of Beach Road, an ambulance waited.

The lifeboat drove in, bows foremost, through the shallows, the point of the bow almost reaching dry sand. The launchers were ready with their balancing poles, which were inserted on either side and held by two launchers on each pole, whilst others placed the skeats—wooden slipboards with loops of rope at each end—under the bows of the boat. The cable from the tractor was attached and began to haul the heavy boat from the water.

As the *Mary Martha Clamp* came clear of the water out on to the hard sand, there was a pause whilst Martin Milner, with a blanket around his shoulders, was handed down the ladder to Tony Douglas.

'Put me down, mister,' Martin said and began to wriggle as he saw his mother running across the sand towards him. 'Put me down.'

Thinking the boy wanted to show his anxious mother that he was all right, Tony set him down on the warm sand and, seeing that he was reasonably steady on his feet, allowed the boy to walk towards the woman.

But the loving, tearful reunion, which Tony Douglas had expected, did not happen.

Thwarted of her revenge upon both boys, Blanche's hysterical anger fell upon

Martin's frail and trembling shoulders. She flew towards the child, hand raised and clouted him across the side of the head, felling the already unsteady little boy to the sand.

Fred Douglas saw his son, Tony, grit his teeth and move towards the screeching woman threateningly. He was beside him in an instant to lay his hand, warningly, on Tony's arm.

'Here, steady on, missus,' Fred spoke up first. 'We know the little lads have done wrong, but they've had their punishment...'

'What the bloody 'ell do you know about it?' She turned on Fred, who smiled sadly at the uncontrolled woman. He watched as Joe Milner tried to take her by the arm and reason with her, but she only struck out at him too, lashing his face viciously.

At that moment Jack Hansard moved forward and scooped the boy up from the sand and carried him to the waiting landrover.

'Where are you takin' him?' Blanche screamed after the coastguard and made as if to follow, but Joe held on to her, fighting her flailing arms and kicking feet. 'Blanche, Blanche, for God's sake.'

The police constable took hold of

Blanche's arm. 'Now look here, love, he needs a hospital check. And your other lad's there. Calm down, missus, and we'll take you there in the police car.'

Blanche pulled her arm from his grasp. 'I ain't ridin' in no bloody police car!' And with that parting shot, she ran, stumbling, up the beach.

Joe sighed heavily. 'Officer, I'd be glad to come to the hospital if you'd be good enough to take me.'

'Of course, sir, come along.'

They turned and followed the landrover making its way up the beach towards the ambulance waiting to take Martin to the hospital.

Macready saw them go out the corner of his eye, but then his full attention was claimed by the beaching procedure.

The lifeboat was hauled up on to the carriage, the chains secured and the tractor swivelled around once more, recoupled and the rescue party moved off up the beach.

Back in the boathouse hot soup and a tea-urn brought in from one of the nearby front cafes—owned and run by Pete Donaldson's parents-in-law, as it happened, where Angie often helped out in her spare time—awaited the crew and launchers, but the work was not done even yet.

The *Mary Martha Clamp*, her carriage and tractor had to be hosed down with soapy water and rinsed again with clear water. The lifeboat was refuelled, the oil level and cooling system checked thoroughly.

Only then, approximately an hour and a half after beaching, could Macready telephone his headquarters at Breymouth to report that the Saltershaven lifeboat was now back on station and ready for service.

Out in the Atlantic the depression continued its steady progress towards the Irish Sea.

CHAPTER 7

'Dad, you remember Howard?'

Her father was looking tired, Julie could see, but to her relief he held out his hand towards her young man and smiled. 'Glad to see you again, Howard.'

'And you, sir.'

As they sat down to their meal, Howard said, 'Would you care for a glass of champagne, sir?'

Macready looked up to see the good-looking young man holding a green glass bottle. He glanced at Julie and saw the blush of embarrassment creeping up her neck.

Smiling inwardly, but keeping his face straight, Macready said, 'Thank you, that would be very nice,' and pushed his glass forward.

Of course it went with the Ferrari and the brand-new sailing-dinghy standing in the driveway, he could see that, but Macready had only ever bought champagne twice in his life—for his wedding and at the birth of his daughter.

Attempting conversation, Howard Marshall-Smythe asked, 'Was it a successful rescue, sir?'

Macready sighed wearily. 'Och, it was one of those times when it leaves a bad taste in the mouth. The rescue itself was successful—one laddie looks in pretty bad shape though. The helicopter took him to hospital.'

'Oh I say, you have a helicopter here as

well, do you?' Howard Marshall-Smythe seemed for a moment impressed.

'Not here, no,' Macready replied. 'We call in the R.A.F air/sea rescue helicopter from a base in Norfolk.'

'Oh.' There was an expressive pause as Howard added, 'I see.'

The silence, whilst they ate, was a little uncomfortable and was not improved by Howard's next remark. 'And you're employed on a full-time basis as coxswain, are you, sir?' Howard laughed as he added, 'It sounds just the sort of job that would suit me. One or two rescues a week and the rest of the time free.'

Macready said nothing. Normally he would not have allowed anyone to escape with such a loaded remark, but this young man was a guest in his house, Julie's guest, and one glance at his daughter's face told him that she was already suffering agonies of embarrassment, knowing as she did how Howard's tactlessness would anger Macready.

It was not so much anger that Macready felt towards this young man and his like, as an incredulity and a kind of sadness that anyone could be so ignorant of the true nature of the lifeboat service of his country.

A service which at any time Howard, or his family, might have to call upon.

The care and attention that Macready lavished on the *Mary Martha Clamp*, on its mechanical and electrical equipment and on the tractor and even the boathouse too, was almost a full-time occupation in itself. Engines and motors could not be left to chance. It was vital they started first time, *every* time. All the life-saving equipment, ropes, pulleys, life-jackets, the breeches-buoy, flares, first-aid supplies and equipment—all had to be in perfect condition at all times.

The coxswain was in daily, almost hourly, contact with his local coastguard, with the Coastal Rescue Headquarters at Breymouth and with Bill Luthwaite, the local honorary secretary of the lifeboat, to say nothing of the publicity side of his work. Because the Royal National Lifeboat Institution was a voluntary organisation, existing only from funds raised from the public, the lifeboat station was open daily throughout the summer and literally thousands of people would climb the wooden steps to look over the *Mary Martha Clamp*. Though they were not allowed on board, they had a good view of the inner workings of the boat and Coxswain Macready was nearly always on hand to answer their hundred and one questions.

There was speech-making, lectures and film shows to give all the year round and throughout it all Macready was on call twenty-four hours a day. At any time, day or night, he could be called out on a service. Never, ever, was there a time in the day when Bill Luthwaite did not know Macready's exact whereabouts.

With great forbearance, Macready changed the subject, at least partially. 'I see you have a sailing dinghy.'

'Oh yes, sir. I bought her last week. Haven't had chance to try her out yet. I was hoping we'd have the opportunity this weekend.'

'Have you had any experience?' Macready asked, careful to keep any sharpness, any sign of anxiety, from his tone.

'Oh yes, sir. I row for my House at the University, and I was telling Julie, as a nipper I used to spend all the hols with some friends of mine who had a boat. Never out of it hardly.'

Macready smiled thinly. 'Well, take care. Julie knows this coast well, of course, but it can be very treacherous.'

Howard laughed again. 'I hear there's a very good rescue service in this area.'

For a dreadful moment Macready felt a shudder pass through him and a shadow cross his eyes like a terrible premonition, like Fate striking a blow at the young man's wisecrack.

Macready laid his knife and fork together and rose from the table. 'Will you excuse me now? I'm away to ring the hospital an' see how that wee laddie is.'

In the hall, Macready dialled the number of the hospital at St Botolphs—the nearest major hospital to Saltershaven. He was put through to the appropriate ward and he asked the sister in charge for news of the boy, Nigel Milner.

'Are you a relative?' the sharp voice asked.

'No, no, I'm not but I was concerned about the wee laddie.'

'Who is that speaking? What is your connection with the boy?'

'It's Macready from Saltershaven, the coxswain...'

He got no further for immediately the woman's tone altered. 'Oh Mr Macready— I'm sorry. I didn't realise it was you.

The boy is in Intensive Care at the moment, but he is already showing signs of improvement since he was first brought in.'

'But you think he will be all right?'

'Oh yes, Mr Macready. If all goes well he should be out of the I.C Unit tomorrow and in the Children's Ward.'

'Good, good.'

The Sister added, 'We've had the mother here...' She paused as if waiting for some comment from Macready. He could well imagine the Sister's reaction to Mrs Milner if the woman had put on the same show at the hospital as she had at the beach. But Macready remained silent. It was not his nature to condemn Blanche Milner. He was a kindly, compassionate man and over the years had seen anxiety and fear play cruel tricks with people's emotions.

'Aye well, I'd be across mysel' to see the laddie, but we've a busy weekend here, ye ken?'

'I do understand, Mr Macready.'

'I'll be in touch again, though. Thank you, Sister.'

'Goodnight, Mr Macready.'

He had replaced the receiver and was

about to go back into the dining-room when the phone began to ring.

'Macready.'

'Mac—it's Bill. There's been another call about a flare seen out on Haven Flats again. This time it came from the police, but again no further information, no name, nothing. Someone just dialled nine-nine-nine and yelled down the phone that they'd seen a red flare out at sea.'

Macready let out a long sigh. 'Eeh, dear, dear. And no one else has seen anything? Have you checked with Jack?'

'Yes. He's on the front now in his landrover taking a look.'

'I'll meet you there—at the end of Beach Road.'

'Right you are.'

Macready poked his head round the dining-room door. 'I'm away to the boathouse. Looks as if our hoaxer's on the loose again.'

'He means you having a busy weekend, Mr Macready,' Howard said.

'Aye, it looks like it,' Macready replied shortly.

Julie was on her feet, 'Oh Dad...' The worried look on her face caught at the big man's heart.

Softly he added, 'Don't wait up, hen. 'Night.'

He turned away and left them together.

Macready reversed his car into the parking-spaces marked in white paint on the left-hand side of the wide Beach Road leading from the fountain to the sands. The road had been extended eastwards beyond the actual promenade, or sea wall, as the build-up of sand pushed the sea farther and farther out. Only in winter did the high spring tides occasionally reach the roadway.

Jack Hansard, binoculars to his eyes, and Bill Luthwaite were already at the end of the tarmacked surface staring out to sea.

'Anything?' Macready asked as he joined them.

'Only the oil-rig lights to the north-east and an odd trawler or two, and the ships moving towards St Botolphs. Here, take a look.'

Macready put the glasses to his eyes and focused them. It was barely dusk yet already the lights were winking out at sea, bright specks on the darkening water.

'Of course we can't see round Dolan's Point from here,' Jack murmured. 'I'd better go down there, I think.'

Macready lowered the glasses thought-fully. 'I really don't know what to say. Let's go back to the boathouse and I'll have another word with the police before you go down there, Jack.'

The three men walked back up the road and turned left towards the boathouse.

Macready dialled the number of the local police station 'Anything else on that report of a red flare?' Macready asked the sergeant on duty.

'Ah yes, Mac. We've been trying to get hold of one of you. About five minutes ago another call came in. A girl's voice this time. Said she'd seen a funny light shoot into the sky over the sea.'

'Did she give her name?'

'No. I asked her where she was, when she had seen it and so on. She replied near the marshes, but when I got to asking her name, she rang off.'

'Mmm.'

'Of course it could be a hoaxer with an accomplice, but you know we do get a lot of people—specially during the holiday season—who report things but don't want to leave their name. They're frightened of getting involved.'

'Aye.'

He turned away from the phone as the conversation ended and looked towards his two friends and colleagues. Then he related the fresh piece of information to them and ended by asking, 'Well, what do you reckon now?'

'It complicates it further now there's been another phone call. And we've no proof it's a hoax—not even this morning's report.'

'Well, we couldna find anything this morning, and we were able to have a good look round the area before we went after those wee laddies. Maybe we should take another look though.'

'I'm not happy about it, but yes, we'll launch,' Bill Luthwaite agreed.

Pete Donaldson was in the bath, soaping his back vigorously with the loofah and singing loudly, the volume intended to make up for the deficiency in the tuneful quality of his voice, when Angie in her nightie and negligee opened the door. 'Pete... Whew, must you have it so hot, it's like a sauna in here.'

'You've just come right, slave. I need my back scrubbed.'

'I'm not here for games...'

'How can you *say* that, wench, dressed like that!' He gave her a wicked look out the corner of his eyes.

'Mr Macready's just rung—there's a service...'

The bath water sloshed from end to end like a tidal wave as Pete shot upright and almost jumped straight out of the bath. The water cascaded from his lean body, soaking the pink carpet. He snatched a towel from the rail and began rubbing himself quickly. 'Angie love, fetch us me clothes. Two pairs of socks and an extra sweater,' he shouted after her. 'Why *do* I have the bath so hot. I'll be frozen out there now,' he muttered crossly to himself.

Angie was back with his sweat-shirt and his navy sweater and holding out a new, thick Aran sweater he hadn't seen before.

'Hey, what's this?'

'I knitted it for your birthday next month, but I think you'd better have it now.'

'Aw, sweetheart. That's lovely.' Pete pulled it over his head and thrust his arms into the sleeves. 'It's great, Angie.' He patted the thick Aran sweater on his

114

chest. 'Smashin'. Thanks, love.'

He gave her a peck on the cheek, put his hands on her waist and spun her round so that she ended up in the bathroom and he on his way out the door. 'I'll thank you properly later.'

'Promises, promises,' she shouted after him, but she was smiling as she picked up the wet towel from the floor and let the water out of the bath. She leant against the side of the bath for a moment watching the water gurgle and swirl. Her smile faded as she whispered her usual little prayer and remembered the coxswain's words on the phone.

'We're a bit afraid it's a hoax, Angela. We reckon that first call we had this morning was one. It could be him again...'

Who, thought Angie, angrily, in their right mind would play such a mean trick. Every time the lifeboat was launched it cost a lot of money—all out of the funds donated. And the crew and launchers and boathouse personnel—all except the coxswain—were unpaid volunteers. True, the actual crew members received a small launch fee but it by no means constituted any kind of wage.

And did the hoaxer realise he could be

actually putting people's lives at risk? Not only the lifeboat crew, but the lives of others who may be in real need when the lifeboat was out hunting a phantom of some sick person's twisted imagination.

Angie sighed. Not that anything she could say would alter her Pete. Like all the rest of the lifeboat crew, it wouldn't even cross his mind not to answer a call—hoax or not!

Deep down she was proud of that fact.

But just let her get her hands on that hoaxer and she'd tell him a thing or two!

As the twin beams of the tractor's headlamps probed the eerie shadows of the beach in the deepening dusk, in a shelter on the promenade two figures clutched each other, hands to mouths to stifle their giggles as they watched the procession across the sands towards the sea.

The coastguard's landrover arrived at the end of Beach Road and the two youngsters drew further back into the darkness.

'Come on, Mel, let's see if we can nick any more flares. We'll keep 'em out there all night!'

Like wraiths they slipped away from the shelter and strolled along the promenade—two seemingly innocent holidaymakers out for an evening stroll.

CHAPTER 8

Karl Schlick, Captain of the West German coaster, the *Hroswitha,* hauled himself up the gangway and stepped on to the deck of his ship, wincing as he did so. It was there again, the gnawing pain in his stomach that refused to go away entirely.

He was a big man, with a craggy face which creased into a dozen wrinkles when he smiled. His blond hair was thinning a little now, but his shoulders were as broad, his arms as strong, as they had ever been.

Ill? He scoffed at the idea. Karl Schlick ill? Never! Whenever the pain threatened to become unbearable, he swallowed a mouthful or two of rum. Deliberately he ignored the fact that he might have something really wrong with him for the first time in his life. Just a little indigestion after years of indeterminate culinary expertise by numerous ship's cooks, he told himself.

He gave his deck cargo of packaged timber a cursory glance. It was lashed with wire, covered with tarpaulins and roped. One of the Turkish deckhands was tying off the last rope. He looked up and grinned at his Captain, showing uneven yellow teeth.

'Iss tight, Cap'n.' Expressively the thin, black-haired deckhand slung out his arm to encompass the packages of timber neatly stacked on the deck.

Schlick nodded. 'It had better be,' he growled in German. The deckhand smiled and nodded and almost bowed at the big man. The Turk could not understand a word of German.

Captain Schlick headed for the bridge.

An hour later, at high water on the Saturday evening, the *Hroswitha*, eighty-six metres long, dead weight 2400 tonnes and with a crew of First Mate, engineer, cook and three Turkish deckhands, nosed its way out of Gothenburg harbour bound for the Port of St Botolphs on the East coast of England.

Schlick opened the bottle of rum he

kept in a locker on the bridge and took a mouthful, savouring the taste. It promised to be an easy trip with nothing much to aggravate his stomach pains.

As the ship reached the open sea and the pain was dulled by the spirit, Captain Schlick handed the helm over to the First Mate, Heinrich Droysen.

Whistling through his teeth the tune at present top of the West German hit parade, the Captain watched Droysen's handling of the ship. This was his first trip as Mate and the first time too with Schlick.

'She takes a bit of getting used to,' Schlick grinned as he watched Droysen's slim hands wrestling with the wheel. Droysen glanced at the Captain, a worried frown on his face.

'It's her fifteen-second roll that does it,' Schlick explained.

When most ships the size of the *Hroswitha* averaged a thirty-second roll, a vessel with one of half that time took some getting used to for someone newly aboard. Relief showed on the First Mate's face. 'Ah, that explains it. I was beginning to think she didn't like me!'

Schlick's hearty laugh rang out and then

he turned to lock away the bottle of rum. With a bit of luck he wouldn't be needing too much of that for medicinal purposes on this trip.

The *Mary Martha Clamp* was a thirty-seven-foot Oakley Class Lifeboat powered by twin 52-horse-power, diesel engines and was sixteen years old. It had been provided at a cost of something over £40,000 by a legacy of Miss Mary Martha Clamp, who, during the three decades from the 1920s to the late forties, had been a leading figure in the Saltershaven community. A wealthy spinster, thin, wiry and energetic, with no family, she had found her vocation in the love of her town and the people of Saltershaven had benefited in diverse ways. During the First World War she had been one of the youngest VAD nurses to go to the Front, and, undaunted, in the Second World War she had driven an ambulance in the coastal area around Saltershaven.

It had been on duty as an ambulance driver that she had first come into direct contact with the lifeboat service. The lifeboat, with Mary Macready's father, Bob Randall, as coxswain, was called out two or three times a week throughout the war years to search for the crews of both allied and German aircraft which had either crashed or ditched within the area of the North Sea patrolled by the Saltershaven lifeboat.

Miss Mary Martha Clamp soon became deeply involved. As soon as word came that the lifeboat had gone on a rescue mission, she could be found sitting at the end of Beach Road, hour after hour, often right through nights of total blackout, huddled in the cab of her ambulance. Often the search was fruitless, the weary crew beached, cold and saddened by the fact that they had not been able to save the crews of the aircraft. Some died of terrible mutilation as the plane crashed. Some drowned and others just died from the dreadful cold of the North Sea. But there were many occasions when the lifeboat succeeded and Miss Mary Martha Clamp would be waiting to take the survivors straight to the nearest R.A.F hospital.

In 1950 Mary Martha found she had leukaemia and had only a year or two to live. It was indicative of this amazing woman's fortitude that her immediate action was to make a will leaving her entire estate of some £47,000 to the

R.N.L.I with instructions that a brand-new and most up-to-date lifeboat should be provided for the Saltershaven station.

Now the self-righting Oakley had all the modern aids—a medium- and high-frequency radio/telephone, a radar scanner, a searchlight, and a day and night signalling lamp plus all the other necessary first-aid and rescue equipment. She was soundly constructed with an oak and teak frame and a hull of mahogany with an alloy top. She was manoeuvrable, easy to handle and steady and Macready had a deep affection for the boat he now 'mastered'. After the war, he had met Miss Clamp but by then she was tired and ill and merely a shadow of her spirited real self. But Macready remembered her and never failed to be thankful for the little woman's generosity that had given Saltershaven such a fine lifeboat.

As he climbed aboard the lifeboat at the water's edge in the gathering dusk, he shouted down to his head launcher, 'Don't wait about, Jeff, we could be all night. Let the lads go home and we'll put a call out for recovery when we're coming in.'

'Okay, Mac.'

Jack Hansard watched the launch from

his landrover and as soon as he could see that the boat was safely away from the shallows he called up the *Mary Martha Clamp*.

'Saltershaven lifeboat, Saltershaven lifeboat, this is Saltershaven mobile, Saltershaven mobile. Do you read me? Over.'

Pete Donaldson's voice over the radio/ telephone pierced the stillness of the night. 'Saltershaven mobile, Saltershaven mobile, this is Saltershaven lifeboat, Saltershaven lifeboat. Loud and clear. Go ahead. Over.'

'...I am now leaving the seafront to go to Dolan's Point to keep a look out from there. Over.'

'...Roger, Saltershaven mobile. Out.'

Whilst Pete reported to Breymouth coastguard the details of the service and the conditions at sea, and requested radio and time checks, Macready headed the lifeboat directly eastwards for a distance of about a mile and a half until it was clear of the sandbank known as the Saltershaven Middle and then he set a southerly course until he came level with the Lynn Well Lanby, the marker buoy all shipping bound for St Botolphs made for. Then he turned starboard on a south-westerly course to bring them to the huge sandbank, Long Sand, on the western shores of the Wash.

For the second time that day, Jack Hansard's landrover sped along the narrow coast road towards Dolan's Point. On his right lay the flat farmlands of Lincolnshire. On his left lay the undulating sand-dunes now given over to a Nature Reserve and beyond that the sea. He met no other vehicle for the road led only to the Point and the Nature Reserve and thence to the marshes. Though the road was quite busy during the days of summer, at night the area was deserted.

The wind whistled across the saltmarshes as Jack Hansard parked his landrover and hunched his collar around his ears and began his search on foot. Away from his landrover he could not keep in touch with the lifeboat and his search was the loneliest.

Aboard the *Mary Martha Clamp* the crew prepared themselves for an all-night vigil. At Macready's request Tony Douglas, the signalman, fired a white flare every fifteen minutes. This illuminated the area of the sea all around the lifeboat and the crew scanned the surface of the water for the few seconds that the flare lit up the sea. Then they waited and watched for an answering red flare, but nothing was to be seen.

Macready kept glancing at the echo sounder as he guided the lifeboat through the Freeman Channel and turned north-eastwards into the St Botolphs Deeps.

The last thing they needed at a busy August Bank Holiday weekend, he was thinking, was a hoaxer on the loose.

'Oy, Mel. Will yer look at this bloody great posh car an' boat parked on this driveway?'

At that moment the front door of the house opened and voices drifted into the night air.

'Eh, watch out, Vin,' Mel hissed. 'There's someone coming.'

The two youngsters ducked down behind the wall and waited, listening.

'Well, just how far is it to the night-club?'

'Not far. Half a mile,' a girl's voice answered.

'Half a mile! Good Lord, and you expect me to walk!'

'Oh Howard, it's not far. Besides, you'll never find a parking-space.'

'Don't tell me this place we're going to

doesn't even have a car park!'

'Of course it has a car park, but at this time of the year the town is packed.'

'Oh well, come on. I suppose we'll have to walk.' His laughter drifted through the night air. 'At least you might let me put my arm round you if we walk there.'

They moved on up the road together, the girl's high-heeled sandals tapping along the pavement.

'Come on—they've gone. Right toff, ain't he?' Vin mimicked Howard's refined tones. 'I say, don't tell me this here place h'ain't even got hay car park! Stuck-up git!' He made a rude gesture into the darkness after the couple, though they could no longer be seen. 'Come on, Mel, let's see if Little Lord Fauntleroy has any flares hidden in this posh boat of his. Keep a look out, will you?'

Nimbly, Vin vaulted on to the trailer and over the side of the *Nerissa* and scrabbled in the lockers in the bows of the boat. 'I'm beginning to know where to look in these 'ere boats now, Mel. Ah, here we are, all neatly stacked away, all ship-shape.' Triumphantly the boy jumped down from the boat. 'Look what I've got, Mel, more pretty lights! Won't his nibs get a shock next time 'ee goes sailing and wants rescuin'? There'll be no bloody flares!'

They leant against each other laughing, then the boy stuffed the flares into the front of his leather jacket and zipped it up. 'Come on, let's get the scooter and go back to the marsh.'

Jack Hansard blew into his hands. It might be August and a Bank Holiday too—but at one o'clock in the morning out here on the marshes it was still damned cold!

He thrust his hands deep into the pockets of his great-coat and turned to go back to his landrover parked near the bridge over the River Dolan about half a mile inland from where the river ran into the sea. As he approached the vehicle he heard the steady high-pitched noise of a scooter coming along the narrow road towards the bridge that led to Dolan's Sands and Haven Flats. The engine noise slowed as the scooter negotiated the bridge and the sharp left hand turn in the road immediately after it.

'Now who is this at this time of night?' Jack Hansard murmured to himself.

The light from the scooter's headlamp

swung in a wide arc across the flat marsh, illuminating for a brief moment the scurrying night animals, the swooping owl, the rippling grass. The light swung and came full upon Jack Hansard's dark-coated figure standing beside his landrover. The machine pulled up, paused, turned, the engine whining as the rider opened the throttle, the back wheel skidding in his haste, and Jack's shout of 'Hey, wait a minute!' was drowned as the scooter bounced back over the bridge and sped away back along the coast road towards the town.

'I bet a pound to a penny that's our mysterious flare,' Jack muttered and reached inside the cab of his vehicle for the radio microphone.

Listening to the coastguard's message, Macready said, 'I think you could well be right, but we'll stay here a wee while longer. We'll go right down as far as Roger Sand and then make our way back up the Deeps and anchor off the Flats until first light. We'll take another look around then. Over and out.'

The disco music in the Nite-Lite Club was loud, the lights flashing, the small dance floor crowded with gyrating bodies.

'Not exactly Annabel's is it?' Howard murmured.

'What did you say, Howard?' Julie shouted above the noise.

'I said, "Shall we dance?" '

Julie nodded and they squeezed on to the edge of the dance floor. In the semi-darkness, in the weird, intermittent lighting, Julie could not see the supercilious expression on Howard's face.

Anchored in the St Botolphs Deeps, east of the Haven Flats, there were few lights to be seen in the velvety blackness of the night and the only sound was the gentle slapping of the waves and the lulling motion of the boat.

Macready and Fred Douglas stayed on deck whilst the other members of the crew snatched an hour or two of sleep under the covered cockpit in the bows.

'What d'you reckon, Mac?' Fred Douglas asked.

Macready's eyes scanned the dark water towards the marshes. 'Since Jack's last message, I think it is a hoaxer, but we'd better stay a while now we are here and be sure.'

Dawn found the crew of the lifeboat stiff and cramped and chilled after what seemed a long night of being able to do very little.

At first light they were pleased to be on the move again.

Still there was nothing and Macready took the lifeboat north-eastwards around the Outer Dog's Head sandbank and towards Saltershaven.

At 0700 hours Breymouth, the coastguard and Macready agreed to call off the search and return to station. The call went out to the launchers for the recovery and the *Mary Martha Clamp* beached a little after a quarter to eight. Pete Donaldson arrived home a little after ten-thirty.

'Angie,' he called as he opened the back door, then he remembered. It was Sunday. She might still be in bed. At that thought, his tiredness fell away and light-footed he sprinted up the stairs and opened the bedroom door and tiptoed in.

The bed was neatly made and turned down, and there was a note pinned to his pillow.

'Sorry, darling, Mum and Dad need help at the café today. It looks like being very busy. See you tonight. Love A.'

Pete groaned and then grinned ruefully. This Bank Holiday wasn't going at all the way he and his lovely bride had planned it.

The tiredness washed over him again. He would shower, he decided, have a bite to eat and then a good sleep ready for when Angie came home tonight...

CHAPTER 9

Mike Harland cycled out to the airfield at 09.30 on the Sunday morning in great spirits. The weather today was perfect for an attempt at diamond height, which had to be a height gain of approximately five thousand metres, over fifteen thousand feet, during his flight. The local meteorological office had confirmed that the forecast was for moderate conditions with a south-westerly wind of twelve to fifteen knots with a warning that cumulo-nimbus and storms were expected in the afternoon but the air would be unstable only to about thirty thousand feet. Perfect for cloud-flying. The extra lift a storm-cloud would provide was just what he needed.

Mike had completed the three tests for his Gold C in May of this year. Now he was moving on to the diamond class. There would be a distance flight of 500 kilometres, a pre-declared course flight of 300 kilometres; but first Mike wanted the height.

Although he had only had some three hundred hours flying experience he was ambitious. The drive and single-mindedness he applied to his studies overflowed into his leisure time. He approached his gliding with that same dedication—he wanted to be the best. It was as simple as that.

Mike grinned to himself as he leaned his bike against the wall of the hanger and went inside to help bring out the club's gliders for the day's flying.

'Morning, Mike,' Toby Wingate greeted him. 'You on winch duty today?'

'Not likely! I was on it an hour yesterday. I'm going for my diamond today,' Mike replied, not pausing to talk but making a bee-line for his own personal preference amongst the club's gliders. This was a Blanik, a silver-and-red Czechoslovakian-built glider, a two-seater with instruments in both the front and rear cockpits. It was used often by the instructors for training, but Mike preferred it to any other sailplane and he wanted it today.

'Could you lend me your barograph again, Toby mate?' he shouted from the back of the huge box-like trailer housing the Blanik.

'I suppose so,' Toby agreed reluctantly. Mike was accepted by the other club members and admired by them, though perhaps a little grudgingly, for the awards he earned and the subsequent kudos for their club, but they resented his unwillingness to take his turn at the less interesting ground jobs.

'It's a perfect day for cloud-flying.' Mike's enthusiasm was infectious and Toby could not help responding.

'It forecasts thunderstorms, you know.'

Mike shrugged. 'All the better.'

Toby capitulated. 'I'll stay by the radio for you if you like, but keep in touch, mind.'

Mike grinned and Toby was won over completely, almost as keen now for him to get the coveted diamond height as Mike was himself. Two more club members, one a girl, joined Toby and Mike to help rig the Blanik and then they hooked the glider on to Toby's car and he towed it across the grass to the east side of the airfield, whilst Mike and the girl walked one at the end of each wing to keep the sailplane level. As on the previous day they were launching from north-east to south-west into the wind.

Twenty minutes later, Mike was completing the daily inspection of the glider as it stood tipped sideways into the wind, one wing resting on the grass and weighted down.

Mike checked that all the pins were in place, he looked over the seat-belts, the cushions and the seat in the cockpit for tears or splits and then he ran his hand the full length of the fuselage and around the outer edge of both wings checking that there was no damage to the metal skin of the glider. He checked the controls and lastly synchronised his own wrist-watch with the clock in the glider. Then he went towards the 'box' to make the necessary arrangements for his flight. The office was where every flight must be recorded and certain badge attempts declared before take-off, and logs completed; where visiting members must complete a form and pay their fees; where even the club members must pay a launching fee each time. From here, too, Toby would keep in contact with Mike by radio.

The blackboard listing the order of flights for the day had been set up and Toby was writing up the names. Mike Harland was listed as having the third launch of the day in the Blanik. He glanced at his watch. Good, with a bit of luck he'd be airborne before eleven.

Toby set and sealed the barograph, which after Mike's flight would have to be returned to Toby unopened for him to verify whether Mike had succeeded or failed. But possible failure did not even enter Mike Harland's mind as he eased his unusually rotund form into the cockpit to begin the more detailed cockpit check. He was wearing two thick sweaters—for with the height came the cold—and the parachute, a must for cloud flying, strapped to his shoulders weighed about twenty pounds.

With Toby's help Mike carried out the cockpit check. He paused a moment bringing to mind the aide mémoire CB SIFT CB.

'Controls,' he said, for the first C. 'Full

135

and free movement and working in the correct sense.'

'Check,' responded Toby.

'Ballast—yes, I'm within the limits for the Blanik. Straps,' he wriggled to ensure that he was securely fastened in, so solidly that he almost felt as if he became part of the sailplane.

 'Instruments—no broken glass and all working correctly and all clearly visible.' With particular care Mike checked the turn-and-slip indicator which was essential for cloud-flying.

'Flaps—set for take off. Trim, yes, operating correctly and set for take off.'

'Check,' came Toby's voice.

'Canopy closed and locked,' Mike murmured, but he opened the small window at the left-hand side. 'Brakes,' he pumped the brakes a couple of times, 'working—closed and locked.'

Through the small open square of perspex Mike shouted, 'Right, cable on, please, Toby.'

Toby now stood at the tip of the port wing, supporting it and holding the glider in a level position. He shouted to someone behind him. 'Nev, can you check Mike's launching hook, please?'

136

'Sure.'

The mechanism for back release and release under tension duly checked Mike waited for clearance from the 'box.'

As they waited, Toby said, 'I say, Mike, don't do what old Bob did yesterday.' He was grinning.

'Why, what was that?' Mike shouted.

'Landed up at a military airfield in Yorkshire somewhere and was clapped in the guardhouse.'

'Good Lord, whatever for?'

Toby shrugged. 'Standard procedure. Lock you up first and ask questions after.'

'What happened?'

'Oh, it was okay when he explained it all. They were very nice, gave him a cup of tea and all that—afterwards. But it gave him a bit of a jolt at first.'

'I bet!'

Mike felt the familiar twinge of excitement as he waited for the moment of take-off. Mentally he went over his preparations once more. The barograph was stowed behind the empty rear cockpit out of Mike's reach during flight. The 750-litre oxygen system had recently been charged and was unused. Close at hand were a pair of thick gloves, a map and a stop-watch which he would need for dead-reckoning navigation.

Mike was not following a particular course from his map as he would have been doing for a distance flight, but it was vital to have a map in order to avoid prohibited areas in his search for lift. In his enthusiasm it was so easy to forget to read his map when his eyes were scanning the cloud formation overhead which would take him higher and higher...

The signal came that they were ready for another launch and Mike said, 'All clear above and behind?'

Toby answered, 'All clear above and behind.'

'Take up slack,' Mike requested and raised his index-finger vertically. The huge lights at the end of the caravan flashed a slow on/off signal and Toby swung his left arm backwards and forwards as if marching, until Mike shouted, 'All out.' Then Toby's signal changed to a similar arm movement but this time above his head, and the lights gave a faster intermittent signal.

Mike felt himself being tugged forward and the glider began to move smoothly across the grass, gaining speed. After only a few yards the glider became airborne and began to climb steeply. At twelve hundred feet, Mike released the cable and below him the tiny parachute opened and gently lowered the cable to the ground.

Immediately Mike found a thermal and banking and turning to the right, he began circling, climbing higher and higher, all the while watching the building cumulus above him as a sign of the thermals waiting for him.

He was on his way.

After being airborne for some ten minutes, Mike called Toby up on the radio. 'Golden Eagle Base, this is Great Awk. Over.'

'How's it look?' Toby wanted to know.

The excitement was evident in Mike's tone even over the crackling radio. 'There's a promising cumulus to the west with a base of about three thousand feet. Here I go! Out.'

He felt the glider sink a little just before it entered the swirling thermal and then the surge of lift began. Banking and turning to the right, Mike worked the thermal, spiralling up and up at a rate of climb of about eight knots until he reached a height of three thousand feet which was, in fact, cloud base. Just as he was about to leave this thermal, he pulled back on the stick and the nose of the glider came up sharply and with a final sudden thrust upwards the Blanik gained an extra two hundred feet. It was a technique Mike had perfected for himself in his quest for height, but each time it was like a high-speed elevator, causing his stomach to heave into his throat and leaving him with a sensation of nausea. But it was worth it, anything was worth it to get that little bit of extra height.

He straightened out into the wind and soared into the clear air. Ahead was another cumulus, bigger than the last. Finding its core, Mike achieved a smooth climb of some five knots and this time he was able to venture right into the cloud reaching a height of some eight thousand feet. This short cloud climb confirmed that all the blind-flying instruments were working correctly and that Mike himself was not out of practice at this type of flying. He came out of this cloud to continue his search for further thermals. There was nothing at present that would take him much higher than he was already. Now he was losing height and soon he found he had sunk below cloud base which had by this time reached four and a half thousand feet.

'Blast!' he muttered and set his instruments for a course heading south-west. It was from this direction that the storm-clouds would come and Mike intended to meet them.

Macready arrived home for a late breakfast just before eleven. Julie—forwarned by telephone—had bacon, egg, sausage and tomatoes frizzling in the pan.

Of Howard Marshall-Smythe—there was no sign.

Julie greeted him. 'Dad—the Sister from St Botolphs rang about Nigel Miller, is it?'

'Milner. Aye, how is he?'

'Out of Intensive Care and in the Children's Ward and doing nicely.'

'Aaah,' Macready gave a long sigh of satisfaction. 'That's good news.' He sat down at the table smiling—a smile that broadened as Julie placed his breakfast in front of him.

'Mmm, this looks good, hen.' Between mouthfuls he asked, 'Any plans for today?'

'Well, I thought we'd take a picnic out this afternoon if it keeps fine.'

'The forecast said thunderstorms this afternoon.'

Julie grimaced, 'Oh well, perhaps we'll have to think of something else.'

There was silence between them. Macready was thinking about the sailing-dinghy, hoping that they were not thinking of using that, but he could not bring himself to voice his fears, not even to Julie. For the first time in their close relationship there was a constraint between them, caused by Howard.

Was that the reason he couldn't quite take to the young man as he would like to have done. Macready was honest enough to question his own motives, but could honestly answer that it was not jealousy of the fact that he was her boyfriend and might come between father and daughter. Macready just could not feel easy with Howard. He had known the time would come when there would be another man in her life—he would not have wanted it otherwise—but if only it could have been someone like young Tim perhaps.

Macready cleared his plate, drank his tea and watched in silence as Julie set a breakfast-tray. He noted the careful preparation, the items placed just so, the

Sunday paper folded beside the plate.

'What on earth is *that?*' Macready could no longer hold back the words as he saw her pouring an unusual type of breakfast cereal into the bowl on the tray.

'Muesli—it's very good for you.'

Did he detect a hint of defensiveness in her tone? Macready murmured, 'Och, you'll no beat porridge for ya breakfast, hen.'

Julie turned to face him and then Macready was relieved to see the impish humour—so like his own—twinkling in her brown eyes. 'Och away to yon bed wi' ye,' she mimicked him.

Macready chuckled and levered himself up from the chair. 'Nay—I'm away back to the boathouse. The visitors were beginning to drift in when I came away.'

Concern showed on Julie's face. 'Oh Dad, you've been out all night. Surely Bert's there, isn't he?'

Bert was an elderly, white-haired man who had been a crew member for twenty years and since his retirement had virtually run the souvenirs stall in the boathouse. He knew as much about the history of the Saltershaven lifeboats as Macready and at every launch Bert could be found

143

weaving his way amongst the watchers on the sands, rattling his collecting-box under their noses and recounting the vivid stories of the dramatic rescues he remembered.

The Lifeboat Institution owed a great deal to all those like Bert, the ones who beavered away behind the scenes—the Service was in their blood.

'Aye,' Macready replied confidently. 'Bert will be there and Tim too I expect.' He cast a sideways glance at his daughter, but she was avoiding his gaze and making a great play of setting the breakfast-tray.

Macready sighed inwardly. 'Dinner at one?'

'Er—well—yes. Yes, Dad, of course.'

'Take care, hen,' he said as he left by the back door.

'And you, Dad,' Julie replied as always.

On the way out to his eight-year-old car, relegated to the kerbside by Howard's Ferrari Berlinetta Boxer, Macready paused to look over the long, almost rocket-shaped model, its nose pressed up against Macready's garage door whilst the back end of the boat trailer was only just inside the gateway. His glance ran admiringly, yet without an ounce of envy, over the red car with its huge tyres on the well-known Cromodaras five-spoke wheels. It looked sleek, very powerful and very new. But the personalised number plate—HMS 4—gave no indication of the year of registration. Macready bent to look in the side window. The plump leather bucket seats were in black and between them was a centre console of controls under the driver's left elbow. On the dashboard Macready could just read the mileage on the clock—four hundred and thirty-one miles. It was this year's model all right, this month's in fact.

Behind the car sat the sailing-dinghy, just as new and sparkling, looking as if she had yet to dip her bows into water.

Macready climbed thoughtfully into his own car. There was certainly money behind this particular undergraduate—there must be well over forty-five thousand pounds all together sitting there on his driveway. And yet...

It was a curiously peaceful morning at the station. Out across the putting-green the beach thronged with people. Macready could hear faintly the shouts and the noise, but here in the boathouse in spite of the shuffle of sandy feet and the muted voices

145

of the visitors, there was a tranquility.

Yet beneath that superficial calm there was always that hint of expectancy, an underlying alert readiness.

The morning was sultry and to the south-west Macready could detect the faint rumble of thunder.

Jack Hansard called in at the station and he and Macready climbed the ladder to the open-sided loft at the seaward end of the boathouse. Through their binoculars they viewed the holiday-makers; the sailing-dinghies; the speed-boat with its water-skier behind; the children and their airbeds playing in the shallows and their indolent parents lolling on the sands.

'Never changes, does it?' Jack Hansard remarked philosophically. 'Whatever we try to do, they persist in taking no notice. Earlier on I caught three swimmers going into the water and the red warning flag was still flying! They'd walked right past the damn thing and never noticed it—or at least if they had they didn't know what it meant.'

'Aye,' Macready agreed. He glanced at his watch. 'Well, I'll be away for my dinner now. Though I'm not sure there'll be any waiting.'

'Oh? Where's Julie then?' Jack asked.

'She's a boyfriend down from college to see her.'

There was a pause and then Jack remarked, 'You don't sound best pleased, Iain.'

'Jack,' Macready felt the need to confide in his friend of many years, 'you know how I've missed my Mary these past years?'

Jack Hansard nodded sympathetically as Macready continued, 'And it's not that I mind my girl growing up, y'ken, even growing away from me, only—I don't know how to talk to her about—about this young man, not like I know Mary could have done.'

'What's the trouble?'

'I canna put my finger on what's bothering me really. It's just this feeling I have. Och, I dunna know. Maybe I'm misjudging the laddie. It's obvious he's from a very wealthy family.'

Jack cast a shrewd glance at Macready. 'It's not like you to judge someone by their wealth—one way or t'other.'

'No—and I'm nay doing this time. It's his attitude, Jack. He's so—so superior. Makes out he knows it all. You know the type?'

The coastguard nodded. 'And really he knows nothing at all, you mean?'

Macready sighed. 'That's exactly what I'm afraid of. He's brought this brand-new sailing-dinghy with him and...'

'Hello there!' They heard the shout from below and Macready turned away to descend the ladder, the moment of a shared confidence lost.

Tim Matthews's face grinned up at him as Macready reached the bottom rung. 'Hello, Mr Macready. Anything I can do for you this morning?'

'Well now, son,' Macready greeted him. Despite the untimely interruption, he was always pleased to see young Tim. 'I was just about to shut the shop and go and get a bite of dinner. Bert's just away home. But...'

'I'll stay, Mr Macready. They're still wanting to come in and take a look. It'd be a shame to close the door on their money, now wouldn't it?' Tim winked and grinned.

Macready laughed. 'All right. I'll be away then. I'd better not be late seeing as we have company.'

'Er—Mr Macready—er, about Julie. I mean this fella from the university. Is

148

it—well, are they serious, do you reckon?'

Macready could detect the underlying anxiety in the boy's voice, even though he was trying to keep the question conversational, as if it didn't really matter. But Macready knew it did. To Tim and to himself.

He didn't know how to answer the lad, but he was never one to evade the truth. 'I honestly don't know, Tim. But I hope not.' He turned away. He didn't want Tim to see the worry mirrored in his own eyes. 'I'll be back within the hour.'

'That's all right, Mr Macready. I'll be here.'

Macready was thoughtful as he went home. He would miss young Tim, and knowing of the lad's keenness to get into the crew, he regretted that he had not been able to give him a trip before he left Saltershaven. Of course the lad had been on practice launches, but that could never be quite the same as a genuine service.

He opened the back door to the smell of roast beef and Yorkshire pudding. Julie was alone in the kitchen.

'Where's...' he was about to say 'his lordship' but thinking better of it said instead, 'Howard?'

Julie banged the saucepan she was holding on to the cooker top with such vehemence, so totally uncharacteristic of his gentle daughter, that Macready winced.

'Gone to play golf. He always plays golf on a Sunday morning,' she told him shortly.

Mildly Macready said, 'Didn't you tell him what time dinner was?'

'He said he'd be back for dinner.'

Macready glanced at the electric wall clock. 'But,' Julie went on, stressing each word, 'dinner to him is six-thirty in the evening, not one o'clock.'

'You should have said, Julie hen. I'd not have minded having it tonight instead of now,' Macready said. 'You should have gone with him...'

'I—wasn't—asked!' she said pointedly.

'Oh,' he said and then again, 'Oh, I see.' He glanced at the window. 'Well, I reckon he could get rained off any time. It's very black over to the south-west and I heard a rumble of thunder as I came home.'

Macready applied himself to the meal Julie had placed before him. He was sorry to see her upset and yet he could not help but feel a stab of relief that although the Ferrari was gone from the drive, the sailing-dinghy was still safely on its trailer outside Macready's front door.

When Macready went back to the boathouse that afternoon Howard had still not returned.

CHAPTER 10

Mike felt a punch of excitement in his stomach. He had been flying for about one and three-quarter hours using thermals but staying below cloud with just the one exception.

Approaching from the south-west and at a rapid pace was a beautiful sight—a massive cumulo-nimbus, black and ballooning out into the shape of a gigantic anvil.

Mike noted down the time—a little after one o'clock—he would need this information for dead reckoning navigation for inside the thunder-cloud he would be flying blind. Then he set his stop-watch going. The forecast had said windspeed would be twelve to fifteen knots but in the storm it could be more. He would estimate on say twenty to thirty knots and that would give him approximately ten minutes in the cloud with a drift of between five and six miles north-eastwards. He was now about twenty miles south of the airfield and about eight or nine miles from the coast. He didn't want to drift too near to the coast—there were no thermals over the sea and he would begin to lose height instead of gaining.

Adjusting his oxygen mask in readiness, Mike entered the thunder-cloud at about five thousand feet and at first his rate of climb was a smooth five knots.

Rain spattered the perspex cockpit cover and then changed to hail which drummed loudly against the canopy. It was like being in a thick fog but as he circled round and round he passed from areas of dark grey to light as the sun pierced the cloud, streaking it with shafts of opaque pale yellow. But the presence of the misty sunlight belied the actual temperature inside the thunder-cloud and at this height. Now delicate lacy patterns of frosting began to build on the perspex hood and glancing out of the side windows, Mike could just see that ice was beginning to form on the leading edges of the wings. He pumped vigorously at the airbrakes every few minutes to prevent the surfaces icing over.

The hail still hammered against the cockpit and the noise of the wind became a high-pitched whistle, and now he could see very little for the canopy was almost completely frosted over. Worse still, the ice was creeping into the cockpit and the faces of the instruments began to haze. Mike scratched away the frost on the artificial horizon and the altimeter. If necessary, he could fly with just these and the electric variometer which still whined comfortingly above the noise of the wind and the hail.

Mike tried to call Toby on the radio but the interference was so bad he could hear no reply and could not be sure whether his back-up team on the ground had even heard him.

At ten thousand feet Mike pulled on his oxygen mask and switched on to medium flow.

Locked in a temperamental thunder-cloud, virtually blind and with only instruments to aid him, he was still climbing. His stop-watch told him he had been in the thunder-cloud for twelve minutes and had climbed seven thousand feet giving an average rate of climb of just under five knots. Blue splinters of static bounced from the metal fittings and prickled his hands and knees. Again he scratched away the frost on the altimeter and saw that he was at sixteen thousand five hundred feet and still climbing. He turned his oxygen supply to full and began clearing the layer of ice away from the compass.

Lightning suddenly illuminated the cockpit and the compass needle spun recklessly and then settled pointing due east. Mike swore under his breath. If his compass were permanently damaged by the lightning, he would have no means of knowing in which direction he was flying. But he was climbing still. Once again he cleared the ice from the altimeter and saw that it registered nineteen thousand feet.

Another shaft of lightning split the sky and the compass went berserk once more. Now Mike could smell the burning from the discharge in the lightning and the thunder was crashing all around. The cockpit of the Blanik was at the centre of a maelstrom of roaring wind, searing light and ear-splitting noise. Half a minute later, the sailplane hit the rapid downcurrent at the rear of the storm and Mike sensed himself hurtling downwards, losing height at an alarming rate. Still the compass needle pointed due east, but Mike assumed that it was irreparably broken and decided to ignore it.

Now the glider began to spin and he fought to control the downward spiral. According to the artificial horizon, the Blanik was spinning as if pivoting on its port wing. Tossed and blown like a feather amid the whirlpool of the thunder-cloud, Mike knew he should not trust his own judgements, his own feelings; sensations in cloud-flying were misleading. Immediately he applied the opposite rudder fully and moved the stick forward steadily. The spinning slowed gradually and the airspeed indicator needle began to rise again. But the sailplane was now diving steeply. Mike now eased the glider out of the dive and levelled the wings by means of the ailerons.

The rapid descent and the resulting spin had left Mike feeling light-headed and more than a little queasy. His stop-watch had been thrown to the floor of the cockpit and appeared to have stopped. His lack of trust in the reliability of the compass robbed him of some of his confidence and, momentarily, he was about to abandon the whole project when, remarkably, the variometer began to whine again, indicating lift. The cockpit had become lighter although he still could not see out because the canopy was covered with ice. The lift was weak now—only about three knots, but it gave Mike time to pull himself together. He flicked his radio switch and repeated his call-sign to Toby.

'Golden Eagle Base, this is Great Awk. Are you receiving me? Over.'

Three times he repeated the message but each time the only reply was the dreadful crackling of interference which filled the cockpit.

'Nev, Nev,' Toby shouted across the stretch of grass between the 'box' and where Nev stood holding the wing tip of a Slingsby Skylark IV awaiting launch. 'Can you come and look at this darned radio? I can hardly hear Mike now.'

'Okay—in a minute when I've finished here,' Nev's voice drifted across the field. Directly above the airfield the sky remained comparatively clear with fluffy cumulus tempting the pilots into the air. To the south the sky darkened and sunlit streaks of rain streamed from cloud base to the ground.

'Reckon we're in for a thunderstorm?' Nev remarked as he came over to where Toby was still fiddling with the radio receiver. Nev turned and watched the glider he had just helped to launch release the winch cable and turn northwards away from the threatening black cloud.

'I dunno what's up with this thing,' Toby muttered, impatience for once evident in his tone. 'Can you do anything with it, Nev? All I can seem to get is a roaring sound.'

'I reckon that storm might by-pass us. It's going out to sea,' Nev answered his own question and then squatted on his haunches in front of the radio. With gentle fingers he eased the dials slowly first one way and then the other. 'I've heard that sort of noise before...' Nev stood up slowly and his gaze went skywards above their heads. He nodded towards the thickening cloud to the south.

'That's the noise of hail drumming on the cockpit. I reckon the damned fool is in that lot!'

Toby's mouth dropped open as he too gaped at the thunder-cloud.

The lift continued steadily for a time and then without warning the visibility darkened again and suddenly Mike felt the glider being sucked up again at a rate of about eight to nine knots. He was confused. Had he turned into the storm again? His eyes felt as if they were bulging and his ears began to hurt and he felt a strange, giddy light-headedness. His thinking was slow and confused. Why did he feel so strange? He made a conscious effort to check his oxygen supply but that seemed to be working okay and there was plenty left.

Up and up he was drawn. A loud crack above his head made him jump violently and look up. It was the canopy contracting in the high altitude. Somewhere inside his head a voice said 'get down, get down'. He must be very high to be feeling like this.

Get down, get down!

He reached forward to scratch away the ice on the altimeter. Had he made it? Had he got his diamond? He ought to be over twenty thousand feet to be absolutely sure.

Suddenly the sailplane lurched and the whine of the variometer stopped. He was plunging, spiralling down, down, down, seemingly out of control in a vicious down-draught. Mike opened the airbrakes to limit his speed to avoid structural damage.

The cloud and the greyness seemed to go on for ever.

He was on the point of throwing open the cockpit and jumping out, hoping desperately that the altimeter, now hazy with frost again, was correct. According to it, he still had some ten thousand feet. The parachute was a comforting lump behind him. Much, much lower now he could hear the ice begin to chip away from the canopy and the wings. Still the glider bucketed downwards.

Suddenly, the sailplane broke out of the cloud. Gently he eased back on the stick and opened the tiny side window to look out.

'Oh my God! The sea. I'm over the bloody sea!' He must have miscalculated very badly. The windspeed must have been far greater inside the storm and he had lost track of the time he had spent inside the cloud. Desperately he craned this way and that. Was there land in sight? Could he make it back to the land. But all he could see was the undulating softness of the water below and to one side the thundercloud he had just come out of.

He flicked the radio switch and his voice was hoarse as he shouted, 'Toby—Toby. Are you there?'

There was no reply, but desperately he continued to broadcast just in case someone—anyone—could hear him. Forgetting all official radio procedure, he just shouted for help. 'Toby—the sea—I'm over the sea. I'll have to jump. No—wait. I can see land to my left. But *miles* away.'

The only reply was a continuous crackle of interference.

He became aware that he was gripping the stick tightly with both hands. Sheer panic surged up inside him and threatened to engulf him, blotting out all reasoned thought and calculation.

Wait—wait! Mike took two deep breaths and then tore off his oxygen mask. Get a hold of yourself, he commanded himself sharply. What he should do was to try to glide westerly into the wind and towards the coastline. Above him the thunder-cloud drifted out to sea, leaving Mike, tossed and buffeted, to try and make land before the height ran out.

He tried to swallow the fear rising in his gullet, tried to concentrate on easing the swooping sailplane in a westerly direction, straining his eyes through the now rapidly clearing windscreen. He was conscious of the fact that the icing still left on the wings was having a drastic adverse effect on the performance of the glider, but as the sailplane passed into warmer air, the ice fell away completely.

Something jogged at his brain. If he was over the sea then he *had* come east—just like the compass had shown him. The storm had blown him off course and instead of trusting his instruments he had preferred to believe them damaged by the lightning.

The hazy outline of the coast was coming nearer, but he was dropping lower and lower towards the water. Again he flicked the radio switch and repeated his mayday message to Toby, but there was still no response.

One thousand feet and now he knew that he could not make land.

'Well, the nearer I can get the better,' he muttered aloud and thought, maybe someone will see me. He tried to concentrate on how to bring the glider down smoothly on to the water, whilst part of his mind tried to estimate how long he would have before the glider sank and how he could get rid of some of his bulky clothing. With his free hand he unfastened his parachute and unzipped his anorak. He groaned aloud as he remembered the extra layers of clothing he had on to combat the high-altitude cold. He'd be a dead weight as soon as that lot became water-logged.

Five hundred feet and the bumpy line of sandhills was so much clearer but still about six miles away. Knowing now that he would have to ditch, Mike checked that the undercarriage was retracted and operated the flaps to try to land as slowly as possible. At the last possible moment, only feet above the waves, he purposely stalled the glider so that it dropped as flat as he could make it on to the surface of the water. But still the impact jolted him, jerking his head in a whiplash movement, his body still held rigidly by the safety harness.

Inside the cockpit the man sat motionless, his head lolling to one side as the sailplane settled into the water.

Miraculously, Toby heard that last desperate message. Though he could not make the glider pilot hear him in return, faintly he had picked up Mike's signal which, though weak and distorted by interference, was coming through.

Toby heard, 'The sea—I'm over the sea.'

'Where, man, where?' Toby yelled into the radio, but it was no use. Obviously Mike could not hear him.

'Nev—*Nev!* It's Mike. He's coming down. Over the sea!'

Neville Grey's mouth dropped open and he just stood and stared for a few precious seconds. 'The sea?' he repeated stupidly. 'What's he doing over the sea, for Christ's sake?'

'I don't know,' Toby almost shrieked. 'What the hell do we do?'

'Ring nine-nine-nine and—and—er—yes, ask for the coastguard.'

Relief flooded through Toby. 'Of course, of course. I should have known.'

Still muttering, he began to gallop across the grass to the nearest telephone. The operator wasted no time in connecting him and the coastguard took his breathless message with calm efficiency, though Toby felt extremely foolish that he could not be more helpful, could not guess where Mike was actually coming down. All he could do was to give the coastguard the time and place of take-off. As he replaced the receiver and leant against the side of the phone booth, he realised that there was nothing else he could do now.

It was all in the hands of the rescuers.

CHAPTER 11

The slate-blue thunder-cloud from the south-west broke over Saltershaven just after two o'clock. The holiday-makers ran for shelter and in a few moments the beach was empty. Tim watched the storm from the boathouse now crammed with people taking refuge from the rain.

Children crowded round the souvenirs table. 'Buy me a toy lifeboat, Mum. I want that toy lifeboat.'

'Dad, I wanna pencil—it's gorra lifeboat on it. Oh an' there's a car sticker. Let's 'ave a sticker for t'car, Dad.'

Above their heads Tim grinned at

Macready. At least the thunderstorm had brought them into the boathouse. Tim served the customers as hands reached out for toy boats and pens, tea-towels and mugs, brushes and rulers, badges and diaries, and the money clinked into the box.

The thunder-cloud covered half the sky, yet all around its edges the sky remained a tantalizing brilliant blue and to the south, the sun shone through the clouds in pale yellow streaks. Hail-stones spattered the roads and pavements and running holiday-makers covered their heads with towels, newspapers, beach-bags, anything they could find. The deckchairs in the gardens were left where their fleeing occupants had been sitting. No customers queued for the miniature railway, or for the rowing-boats or for the clock-golf, and in the children's play park, the swings moved idly, emptily, to and fro, the toddlers tricycles were strewn along the pathways abandoned at drunken angles. The hail pitted the sand beneath the climbing-frame and drenched the seats of the red rocking-horse and the see-saw.

The hail turned to a fine rain and then ceased. As the thunder-cloud passed over the town and rolled out to sea, the sun shone down again and the holiday-makers emerged once more.

Jack Hansard received Toby's message at two forty-six. The lifeboat secretary approved a launch and Macready began his telephone calls to his crew. Tim Matthews was away and running across the road, over the railings and across the wet grass of the putting-green to the circular slab of concrete to fire the maroons. One. Two.

As the flares snaked into the sky and cracked almost in unison with the thunder out at sea, the lifeboat collecting boxes in the pubs and clubs along the seafront were rattled under the noses of the lingering drinkers.

'Just your coppers we ask for,' the landlords said. 'No, madam, no silver, thank you. Just whatever copper you have in your purse or pocket.'

'Christ!' muttered one man. 'I just won all this—a quid's worf—on the slot machines!' But good naturedly he grinned and fed it into the box.

'Many thanks, sir,' the barman said. 'You never know when it might be your turn to need the lifeboat launched for you!'

Pete Donaldson was having a most peculiar dream. He was driving a fire-engine, the bell clanging loudly in his ears. He was driving up the main street through Saltershaven, round the fountain and straight down Beach Road and on to the sand and straight into the sea, the bell still ringing only it wasn't really a clanging fire-bell, more like a telephone bell.

Pete surfaced from the depths of sleep to find that the insistent telephone bell was a reality.

Another service!

The launch was one of the fastest on record.

Macready never sacrificed smooth efficiency for hectic, uncalculated rush, but occasionally the very urgency of a particular service gave impetus to each and every man. All the practice launches paid off, all the teamwork came together in perfect harmony, and the lifeboat was in the water in a space of time little short of miraculous.

This was one such time.

Each member of the crew knew that the glider would sink in minutes. If the pilot were trapped, or sick, or injured, he would go down with the plane. Even if he managed to get out of his craft before it sank, if he had no life-jacket—and glider pilots scarcely ever envisaged being plunged into the sea—the weight of his water-logged clothes would soon drag him under.

The *Mary Martha Clamp* entered the water thirteen minutes after leaving the boathouse, despite the fact that it was low water. At that precise moment, Jack Hansard received a message from the police that a holiday-maker had reported seeing a light plane go down into the sea.

Two hundred yards out to sea, Pete called up Breymouth coastguard on the radio/telephone and reported the conditions at sea, stated that the crew list was as normal and asked for the usual radio and time checks.

Jack Hansard's landrover, with 'H.M Coastguard' in black printing on a yellow background, appeared at the end of Beach Road. Over the radio, still crackling with interference from the storm, he relayed the recent message to Coxswain Macready. '...A report has been received of a light plane ditching about five or six miles out and from the details given, I estimate he's somewhere in the region fifty-three degrees ten minutes north, zero degrees thirty minutes east. Over.'

'Saltershaven mobile, this is Saltershaven lifeboat. Proceeding on course bearing zero six zero. Out.'

The lifeboat plunged through the choppy seas at a maximum speed of eight and a half knots and Pete Donaldson tuned in his radar and sat hunched over the screen.

Mike Harland became aware of the curious motion of the glider, a gentle rocking, of a cold wetness about his legs and the sound of lapping water. He moaned as one waking from a deep slumber and moved his cramped limbs. He opened his eyes and blinked rapidly.

'Christ!' he muttered and panic surged up inside him. The glider in which he was still tightly strapped was sinking. His numb fingers began to grapple with the fastenings but at the same time in his fear he was straining against the straps, making it harder for the release catch to work. He felt the bile rise in his throat. Fear or sea-sickness from the rocking motion of the sailplane? He couldn't tell. All he knew was that he must get out.

He—must—get—out!

He heard a click and felt the straps loosen. The water was already lapping over his knees as the nose dipped beneath the surface. Mike unlatched the canopy and threw it open. Then he tried to heave himself up, but the glider rocked alarmingly. Levering himself up by his hands on either side, he drew his legs up until he was squatting on the seat. The water now covered the seat and washed at his ankles. He sat on the top edge of the back of the seat and wriggled out of the parachute harness and tossed the package into the water. All the time the glider rocked and rolled with the swell of the seas, threatening to pitch him into the water.

He was pulling off his anorak and thick sweater when a wave, bigger than the rest, smacked against the side of the sailplane. Mike lost his precarious balance and felt himself falling, his arms still awkwardly pinioned half in, half out of his coat. He plunged forward into the water.

It was only a matter of twenty minutes after the launch before Pete Donaldson, his gaze fixed on the blipping screen said, 'Cox'n—there's an object in the water about two miles away.'

Macready took a quick look at the screen and then altered course slightly three degrees to port and reached for the binoculars. The lifeboat sped on at full throttle.

Fred Douglas was already in the bows and the rest of the crew in their usual positions when they all saw, about half a mile away, the tail-fin of the Blanik rise in the air and then slowly slip beneath the waves.

The lifeboat approached the spot where they estimated the glider had disappeared. Macready slowed right down and anxiously all eyes scanned the water around the boat.

'God—if he were still trapped in the bloody thing!' Fred muttered to himself, but no sooner were the words between his lips than he raised his voice and shouted, 'There, Cox'n, to port. Is that him?'

Fred Douglas might be the oldest, except for Macready, aboard the lifeboat, but his eyesight was probably the best. Years of searching for objects out at sea had shown him what to look for and how to look.

Macready eased the lifeboat in close to the dark shape in the water.

'It's him right enough!' Fred said and signalled to Macready, directing him to inch closer and closer.

The pilot was clutching the packaged parachute which was giving him a little buoyancy but he was only semi-conscious and a bad colour. Each wave lapped into his open mouth and he could hardly keep his nose and mouth above water.

Tony Douglas and Chas Blake climbed over the side of the lifeboat and down the scramble net. In unison they reached down towards the man in the water hooking their hands under his armpits.

'One, two, three, lift!' Tony said and together they heaved him upwards. But the weight of the pilot's sodden clothes, the dead-weight of his helpless body, was almost too much even for the two fit young lifeboatmen.

'Again,' Tony gasped. 'One, two, three— *lift!*'

They hauled him on to the net and then heaved him up once more whilst from above Phil Davis and Alan Gilbert pulled him over the gunwale. Swiftly they carried him to the bows and as Tony and

Chas came up over the side, Macready turned the lifeboat full circle and headed for home at top speed.

In the for'ard cockpit Phil and Alan attended to the unconscious glider pilot. After clearing as much water as possible from the man's lungs, Phil started to give him artificial respiration whilst Alan prepared to insert the Brook Airway equipment into the casualty's mouth.

Pete was busy on the radio sending a message to the coastguard. '...Request ambulance standing by to receive casualty. ETA approximately thirty minutes. Over.'

When they beached the launchers were still waiting for them on the shore. This time, when they had known it was likely to be a short service, the launching crew had remained on the beach. As the lifeboat approached the shallows, pale, hesitant sunlight filtered through on to a drenched landscape and the launchers made ready to beach the boat. The tractor positioned the carriage at right angles to the water's edge and the tow-rope was attached. The tractor, engines revving, began to haul the boat up on to the beach, the water from the ballast tanks flooding on to the sand.

Carefully, the glider pilot was passed

down from the lifeboat warmly wrapped in blankets and a plastic sheet and strapped to the stretcher. He was a better colour now and had regained consciousness. Jack Hansard's landrover approached the lifeboat, turned and reversed. Chas Blake and Pete Donaldson placed the stretcher in the rear of the vehicle.

In a hoarse voice that scarcely seemed to be his own, Mike croaked, 'Thank you, thank you.'

Chas raised his hand in acknowledgement and smiled. 'You'll be all right, mate.'

As the crew watched the landrover move steadily up the beach towards the waiting ambulance, Fred Douglas was saying to Macready, 'I thought he was a goner when we pulled him out of the water, but Chas and Alan brought him round.'

'Aye,' Macready agreed. 'We only just got there in time.'

The launchers began their methodical placing of the wooden skeats, running in pairs, each carrying the board by a loop of rope at either end from the stern of the boat to the bows as the *Mary Martha Clamp* inched forward towards the iron roller skeat and then on to the rear of the launching carriage itself.

Thunder still rumbled in the distance, way out at sea, as Macready guided his team. The bows rose and the boat slid up the ramp and on to the carriage, the restraining chains were secured and the sand cleared of all the beaching gear. The tractor released, swivelled round and was coupled to the towing gear. The small trailer carrying all the skeats, ropes and poles was attached to the rear of the carriage and the whole party moved off up the beach towards the roadway, the small band of interested holiday-makers parting to allow the lifeboat through.

Back at the boathouse the crew and launchers had hot soup and tea and then began the work of hosing down the boat.

At a little after five-thirty Macready telephoned his RNLI headquarters to report that the Saltershaven lifeboat was back on station and once more ready for service.

In the hospital Mike Harland was comfortable, glad to be alive and grateful to his friends at the Gliding Club and to the crew of the *Mary Martha Clamp*. Thanks to them all, there would be another day.

Ironically, unknown to Mike, eleven

fathoms under the sea the barograph trace showed that during that last strong thermal carrying Mike high in the cumulo-nimbus, when his instruments were out of action in the storm and the glass iced over, he had topped a height of twenty-seven thousand feet. He had indeed earned his diamond award, but could not prove it.

Somehow, though, it didn't seem quite so important now.

Before going home, Jack Hansard drove out to Dolan's Point again. As the sun slipped down behind the Lincolnshire Wolds to the west, along the coast road he passed a few cars coming back towards the town, their occupants having spent an afternoon at the Nature Reserve following the paths through the marshes and along the beach, exclaiming over the names of the marsh plants, clearly labelled, listening to the grasshoppers, watching for the different species of bird.

From behind a clump of elderberry bushes near the bridge, the two youngsters, three flares already in their hands, saw the landrover cross the bridge and take the road towards the flats.

'Come on, Mel, we'd best leave it

176

tonight. I reckon he's goin' to keep watch.'

'Aw, can't we wait a bit and see, Vin?' the girl whined in disappointment.

'No—besides, I'm tired. Come on, let's get back to the tent.' He put his arm around her.

'But we're off home tomorrow night. We won't get another chance.'

'We can 'ave another go tomorrow. Mebbee if 'ee sees nothin' tonight, he'll not bother in the day time.'

'S'pose you're right.'

Before Jack came back across the bridge, the scooter had disappeared towards the town.

Macready's last act before he left the boathouse in the evening was always to reset the barometer in his office.

Even before he had reached his home that Sunday evening, the level of the mercury in the barometer had begun to drop by an imperceptible fraction.

Out in the Atlantic the depression deepened to 984 millibars and moved towards Valencia.

The detailed weather forecast broadcast at fifteen minutes past midnight said, *'...winds mainly south-westerly four, locally six, increasing six, locally gale eight soon...*'

Amidst the flashing lights and the blaring music of the Nite-Life's disco, the last thing Howard, or, for that matter, Julie, was thinking about was the midnight weather forecast.

And after thirty-eight hours on duty Macready was asleep.

CHAPTER 12

It had been a busy Bank Holiday Monday morning at the boathouse. Too blustery for sitting on the beach, the holiday-makers had come looking for entertainment on the foreshore: the amusement arcades, the putting-greens, the bowling-greens, the kiddies' corner, the boating-lake and the lifeboat station. They had streamed into the boathouse to gain ten minutes or so out of the wind that whipped up the sand into their eyes. They studied the pictures on the walls of the present and past crews, read of the brave rescues over the years but could not grasp in those few idle holiday moments the anguish, the courage and

178

sometimes the suffering that lay behind those rescues.

'Four lives saved.'

'Three lives saved.'

Just the bare facts giving nothing about the turbulent emotions of fear and hope and final, joyful, success.

Macready stood by the table of souvenirs watching the visitors as they climbed the wooden steps to the platform level with the side of the lifeboat. They leaned over the rail peering into the illuminated interior of the boat, asking questions, pointing, marvelling. Then down they clattered, sometimes to make their purchases of souvenirs, often to drop coins into the lifeboat-shaped collecting-box and then out again on to the sea-front in search of fresh amusement.

' 'Morning, Mr Macready.'

'Hello there, Tim.'

Tim Matthews jerked his head backwards towards the sea. 'Bit blustery today out there. There's one or two out in boats, and, would you believe, a wind-surfer. Reckon he'll spend more time in the water than on it!'

Macready laughed. 'Aye. No doubt Jack's got his eagle eye on them all.'

'Like me to take over for you while you get your dinner?' Tim asked.

'Aye, if you would, son. Though I'm not sure if there'll be any waiting for me. Julie was away to a disco when I got hame after the service last night—and I left this morning before they—she was about.'

There was an uncomfortable silence between them. Tim scuffed the floor with the toe of his training shoe, his thumbs hooked in the tight pockets of his denims.

They were both thinking about Julie— and the boyfriend!

'Aye, well,' Macready sighed. 'I'll be away anyway, an' see what's to do. See you...'

The phone shrilled in Macready's office and he broke off to go and answer it. He came back a few minutes later, his craggy face wreathed with smiles, a twinkle of mischief in his hazel eyes. 'Och, now I've heard it said that "it's an ill wind..." Young Phil, now, he's fallen off a ladder trying to paint his house—and broken his arm.' He paused and Tim looked puzzled.

'I don't get what you mean.'

'Well now, son. If we should get

180

a service this busy Bank Holiday'—he nodded towards the scudding clouds—'and with this weather, well then, I shall be a crew member short, now won't I?'

Tim drew breath sharply. 'Do you mean...?'

'Aye, if there's a service, Tim, you'll be in the crew.'

Tim's eyes glowed. 'Aw, thanks, Mr Macready. Thanks.'

Macready patted the young fellow on the shoulder.

In the locked office, the mercury in the barometer sank a little lower.

The depression was centred over the Irish Sea and moving rapidly north-eastwards.

When Macready pulled up outside his house he saw that the driveway was completely empty.

Howard's shining car and the trailer and the boat were gone.

'Well, and what are we supposed to do now?' Howard asked sarcastically. He had parked the Ferrari and the trailer at the end of Beach Road as near to the sand as he could and was now standing facing the expanse of beach stretching between himself and the water's edge. Although the tide had only been on the ebb for about an hour, the distance still looked enormous to Howard.

Julie laughed. 'We unhitch the trailer and I go and ask Sandy to tow us down to the sea.'

Howard's expression lightened. 'Oh great! For one terrible moment I thought we were expected to lug the blasted thing all the way to the sea!'

'We're not quite as antiquated as that.'

Julie turned away and busied herself collecting their gear from the back of the car in readiness for stowing it under the foredeck of the dinghy.

Howard stretched and flexed his muscles. 'Right then. Off you go and find this tractor chappie.'

Obediently Julie turned and began to walk towards the Saltershaven Sailing Club's compound, a square of beach above high water mark where the club's boats and gear were kept. She glanced back once over her shoulder to see Howard bending over the tow-bar fiddling with the mechanism.

'Hi, Sandy.'

'Hello, Julie.' He grinned at her. 'You 'n' Tim after borrowing me boat, are you?'

The faint tinge of pink in Julie's cheeks deepened a little. 'Er—no. It's—I mean—I'm not with Tim. Not today.' She flung her arm out to indicate Howard and his car and boat at the end of Beach Road. 'I'm with—a friend I met at college. He's brought his own boat and I was just wondering if you'd give us a tow down to the water, please, Sandy?'

Sandy frowned, his eyes half-closed as he squinted beyond Julie towards Howard and his car and boat. 'By heck, that's a posh effort. A Ferrari, isn't it?'

'Yes.'

Sandy looked back at her. 'Tim got his nose pushed out of joint then?'

'I don't know what you mean, Sandy.' The pinkness deepened. 'Tim and I have been friends from childhood and that's all. Why, we're more like brother and sister than...' Her voice petered out in embarrassment.

For a moment Sandy's pleasant face was sober and his steady gaze was on her face. 'You reckon?'

'Yes.'

Then he shrugged and turned away towards the tractor. 'Oh well, must be me that's got it all wrong.'

For a few moments Julie stared after him, then slowly she returned across the sand towards Howard whilst behind her the roar of the tractor engine drowned the shrieks and shouts of the children playing nearby.

Carefully, Sandy inched his tractor amongst the holiday makers who had braved the windy beach, wary all the time of the tiny, darting figures of the children so intent on their games that they could be totally unaware of the tractor.

Minutes later the *Nerissa* was being towed towards the sea with Howard and Julie jogging across the sand behind it.

'Gad, you have to be fit to live here, don't you?'

Julie's laugh bounced across the breeze. 'That's one thing we're not short of at Saltershaven—good fresh air!'

She was unaware of Howard's cynical glance as she flung her arms wide to encompass the beach, the sea, the sky—the place she loved. She closed her eyes and lifted her face, glorying in the feel of the salty breeze on her skin.

Sandy drew up on the wet sand close to the water's edge, switched off the engine and in one lithe movement jumped down from the tractor. 'Rigging it on the trailer?' he queried.

Julie turned towards Howard who shrugged his shoulders.

'It would be easier, I think,' Julie volunteered.

Howard and Julie began to remove the fittings and sailbag from the interior of the *Nerissa*. Sandy stood, arms folded, watching them, making no move to help at all. Julie glanced at him, but Sandy's eyes were on Howard. Julie sighed, thinking of all the times when Sandy had willingly loaned Tim and her his own boat, and helped them to rig and launch it.

Now he had set himself apart from them, watching Howard Marshall-Smythe's every move, his mouth tight with disapproval.

Julie loosened all the ropes securing the dinghy to the trailer and then stood in the boat whilst Howard struggled to raise the mast. It required more knack than physical strength, but Howard seemed to be lacking in both. Still Sandy made no move to help and Julie was convinced he was smothering his laughter. She guided the heel towards the step and then shouted to Howard, 'Toss it up now.'

'What do you think I am, a fancy caber-tosser in a skirt?' In the heat of the moment, Howard was obviously unaware of his implied insult to Julie's Scottish father.

The mast rose and was slotted into position and Julie caught and held it. Howard, breathing hard, stood a moment.

'Come on, then,' Julie shouted. 'I can't hold this for ever.'

'I'll do it, Julie,' Sandy's quiet voice answered her and he moved forward, evidently unable to keep up his pretence of indifference when he saw her struggling. After all, he had no quarrel with Julie, even if he did feel a bit peeved on Tim's behalf. Swiftly Sandy secured the two side shrouds and the forestay.

Howard had unrolled the jib sail on the foredeck and shackled the head on to the jib halyard and was about to hoist it when Sandy said, 'Er, excuse me, mate, but you should pass your jib sheets outside the shrouds.'

'What?' Howard paused, his grip tightening on the sheet in anger. His eyes flashed towards Sandy. 'Mind your own damn business, will you?'

'Hey, Howard,' Julie cut in. 'Sandy's a friend of mine, and besides...' she added, eyeing the sheets under dispute, 'he's right.'

Howard released the sheet and the sail slithered down into a crumpled heap. He all but pouted like a spoilt little boy. 'Do it yourself then,' he muttered.

'It is very easy to get it wrong,' Julie tried to say soothingly and picked up the sail.

Howard moved away and as soon as he did, Sandy was at her shoulder. 'I'll give you a hand, Julie.'

Under his expert hands the jib was soon rigged and then together they attached the main halyard to the mainsail while a few feet away Howard was fiddling with the rudder.

'Julie,' Sandy said in his soft voice as he stretched the foot of the mainsail along the boom. 'Just how much *does* he know about sailing?'

Julie kept her eyes averted from Sandy's questioning look, busying herself inserting the three battens into the sail. 'Oh, he's done a lot of sailing, but this boat's brand-new, perhaps he's not rigged this type before.' But somehow the confidence was missing from her tone.

Sandy tensed his mouth, biting back the retort that the rigging of one sailing-dinghy was not so very different from any other type of equivalent size. All he could say was, 'Well, take care anyway.'

Julie looked up at him now, her merry eyes smiling once more. 'I'd better. It wouldn't look very good if the lifeboat had to be launched for the coxswain's daughter, would it?'

But, strangely, there was no responsive grin from Sandy. Soberly, he murmured, 'Don't tempt Fate, Julie love.'

But Julie had turned away to fasten the mainsheet on to the port side of the transom and he could not be sure whether she had heard him or not. As she continued to thread the mainsheet through the pulley hanging from the end of the boom and back through the single pulley on the starboard side of the transom finishing with a figure-of-eight knot in the end, Sandy fitted the boom into the gooseneck and hauled the mainsail up a few feet until after the boat was afloat.

Julie stowed their picnic hamper and

other gear under the foredeck. Howard was still busy with the rudder and tiller.

'Have you checked the bungs?' she asked him.

'No. You do that.'

'Okay.'

That done, out of habit Julie took a final look around the boat, checking on the buoyancy-bags and that all the sheets were free-running and the halyards secure. She noticed that Howard had left the rudder blade too far down, in danger of being snapped off when they launched the boat. She opened her mouth to point this out and then closed it again. Better not cause any more trouble, she thought, and silently adjusted the blade herself.

Julie straightened up and stood looking at the boat. 'Well, I think we're about ready now to launch her.'

Sandy stood back too, his gaze roving—not without a trace of envy—over the sailing-dinghy. Noticing the expression on Sandy's face, Howard said, 'Well, what do you think of her?' Howard's good humour was restored by Sandy's obvious admiration of his boat. But all Sandy would allow himself to say to Howard Marshall-Smythe was, 'She's all right.'

Then his eyes narrowed as he nodded towards the *Nerissa*. 'Julie says she's brand-new.'

'That's right. I only got her last week.'

'Well—if this is your first time out in her, you'll not know how she handles. And this coast isn't the best of places to try her.' He turned toward Julie again. 'You know what it's like half a mile out with an offshore wind? You can suddenly hit a maelstrom.'

Julie nodded. 'Yes. I know, Sandy. But we're only going just up and down the coast, we'll keep close inshore. By the way, what do we owe you for the tow?'

Now Sandy laughed. 'Oh, I reckon the Sailing Club can stand you a free tow after all your dad does for our members when they get themselves in deep water!'

Julie smiled at his pun. 'Well, if you're sure...?'

'Quite sure, Julie. Mind how you go, now.' He nodded towards the sea. 'It could get rough further out. I reckon we're heading for a blow.'

She heard Howard's guffaw. 'Nothing like a good stiff breeze for yachting.' He made it sound as if sailing was a daily activity for him.

190

Sandy ignored his remark, but it was obvious that it had not gone unnoticed as he gave Julie a brief nod and said, 'Right, shall we get her into the water?'

At once Howard said, 'I'll stay aboard and fix the rudder and tiller as soon as you get her in.'

Sandy raised his eyebrows but said nothing. Julie was busy releasing the lashings that secured the boat to its trailer and did not appear to have heard. Together Sandy and Julie unhooked the trailer from the rear of the tractor and pushed it into the water until the hull floated freely. Julie held the bows at right angles to the offshore wind whilst Sandy heaved the trolley back out on to dry land.

'Shall I take the trailer back to the compound?' he shouted to her but before she could answer Howard said, 'Oh thanks, old chap. Put it near my car, would you?' Howard turned away and began to haul up the mainsail.

For a moment the amiable Sandy stared at Howard's back. Then, without another word, he re-hitched the trailer to his tractor and drove away up the beach.

As Julie fastened her life-jacket around

191

her, she said, 'We should be all right if we keep to within half a mile of the shore. It's comparatively sheltered for that distance. Beyond that, with this offshore wind, it wouldn't be safe. Howard—your life-jacket.'

'What? Oh don't fuss, Julie. I don't need that thing on, especially if you're planning to keep us pussy-footing around in the shallows.' There was an edge of sarcasm to his tone.

'Howard, you need your life-jacket on,' Julie persisted.

'Look, I'm a strong swimmer...'

'It makes no difference if you could swim the Channel. If you end up in that sea today, you'll need a life-jacket. Besides, you're wearing a dark sweater so you need something on that can be seen easily if you're in the water.'

'I've no intention of being in the water.'

'And whilst we're on the subject, you'd have been better in shorts, not slacks. They'll end up saturated round your legs.' Julie herself was wearing shorts and a warm, lemon sweater.

For a moment they glared at each other, but Julie was determined not to give way on a matter of safety—she had been too well-trained—even if it angered Howard.

Suddenly he laughed and capitulated with good humour. It had been these swift flashes of charm that had captivated Julie when she had first met him. 'Oh all right, I'll wear the blessed thing, but only to stop you nagging me.'

Julie glanced seawards, narrowing her eyes, watching the choppy surf over the Saltershaven Middle, the sandbank lying parallel to the shore about half a mile out.

For a brief moment she hesitated. Instinct told her that today needed experienced sailors and she was beginning to be more than a little unsure of the true extent of Howard's experience. But he had assured her that he had spent a lot of time sailing, surely...?

The wind had caught the mainsail and it was flapping furiously before Howard had secured it. 'Come on, Julie, lend a hand, old thing.'

Burying her apprehension, Julie moved forward to help him.

The offshore wind caught the sails and they drifted sideways in a south-easterly direction. Soon they were far enough offshore to bring the boat about and to begin sailing in a southerly direction on a reach parallel to the shore with the wind blowing at right-angles to the boat, the centre-board half up and the sails well filled.

'Right, I'm helmsman. You'll have to crew, Julie.'

Howard, seated starboard with his back to the wind, the sails to port, was in command at the helm, the tiller in his left hand, the mainsheet in his right. It was Julie's task to move about the boat to carry out all the jobs as crew: to keep the jib roughly parallel to the mainsail and to act as ballast to help Howard keep the boat level.

'My word,' Howard laughed, the breeze catching his words and tossing them overboard. 'This is the life. Do you know, I'd forgotten how jolly this sailing lark is. Come to think of it, I've never been on the sea before, only on the Lakes. This is great, I must say.'

With the wind drumming the sails, the sheets humming and the waves smacking against the boat, Julie, struggling with the jib, did not hear what Howard had said.

CHAPTER 13

They sailed the *Nerissa* southwards, parallel to the shoreline for a couple of miles, then, by pulling up the helm and slackening off the sheets, the boat turned seawards away from the wind.

Howard, ducking beneath the boom, brought the mainsail round to starboard and slackened the mainsheet. The jib remained on the port side and Julie withdrew the centreboard fully. Now they were running free before the wind.

Half a mile out to sea, they turned on a port gybe, reaching northwards now, then two miles further on going about and beating to windward in a zigzag pattern to complete the rectangle and bring them back almost to their starting-point. Then once more Howard swung the tiller, switched sides, brought the mainsail across to port, whilst Julie tussled with the jib, yet again reaching southwards.

Above the thrum of the wind, Howard shouted, 'Is there anywhere along the coast we can pull in for the picnic? That bottle of Asti must be about to pop with all this shaking.'

'We'll moor at the Haven. It's about a mile and a half down the coast from where we are now.'

The Haven proper of Saltershaven was some two miles down the coast from the town itself. As the houses petered out and the golf-links ended, the land gave way to sandhills, saltmarshes and mud flats which had become a nature reserve and bird sanctuary. Through this the River Dolan meandered towards the sea, its mouth just south of Dolan's Point, the final promontory of land before the ground became the treacherous marsh which bordered the Wash.

As they reached the outer marker, Julie looked towards the shore to see the flocks of birds wheeling and swooping against the white and grey clouds scudding across a fitful sun. Beneath them the green marram grass, which grew in abundance on the saltmarsh, moved in gentle waves in the wind.

'Do you know if it's deep enough for us to get there?' Howard shouted, as the red-and-white entry marker came into view.

'Should be—it'll be low water any time, but it should still leave us enough draught.'

Julie, busy with the jib in readiness to tack to starboard, missed seeing Howard's eyes cast heavenwards in an exaggerated expression of boredom of her use of the language of sailing. 'Just tell me—in plain language, if you don't mind—can we get far enough up river to moor at a decent place?'

Julie glanced at him. 'Yes,' she said shortly.

'Good,' Howard said. 'That's all I asked for—not a lecture on sailing terms!'

They passed by the yellow-topped beacon and then followed the series of port and starboard buoys. Then the markers became taller as the narrowing channel was outlined by slim poles, a can on the port hand and a cone on the starboard hand. A sharp bend to port was quickly followed by an equally sharp bend in the opposite direction.

'Good God—where the hell are you taking us?'

'Nearly there,' Julie panted. 'One more bend and we're there.' And indeed as they passed by the starboard markers set to mark the almost right-angled turn, Howard saw the moorings along the river-bank.

'Thank God for that!' he muttered. The River Dolan curved gently through the marsh towards the sea, with green grassy banks on each side. Every so often mooring-posts were set and wooden step-ladders gave access to the banks.

'This'll do,' Howard said and without warning he swung the tiller sharply so that the boat almost hit the bank and Julie lost her balance.

'Hey—mind what you're doing.'

'Oh, sorry, old thing.'

He tied up the boat and leapt up the steps to stand on the bank above her, gazing at the scenery, whilst Julie let down the sails completely.

'God, but it's flat!' Howard's voice floated down to her. 'Flat and un-interesting!'

Julie clambered up the steps to stand beside him. 'Flat it may be,' she retorted, 'but uninteresting—never!' She flung out her arm to the right. 'All this area is a nature reserve. It just teems with life. We ring birds here that end up all over Europe—even Russia...'

Howard held up his hands, palms out-wards as if to fend her off. 'Oh spare me a geography lesson, darling, please. Come on, let's get the picnic hamper up.'

They found a sheltered spot a few yards away from where they had moored the boat. They crossed the road leading to the car park from the bridge over the river. Turning left, towards the sea the marsh was dotted with sand-dunes and behind one of these it was sheltered from the westerly wind.

Howard opened the bottle of sparkling white wine with a loud bang, the bubbly liquid flooding over the top. He laughed, 'There, I bet you've never feasted like this before out here, Julie.'

Julie bit into the smoked-salmon sandwich which Howard had insisted was the only thing he could eat at a picnic.

'No, you're quite right, I haven't.' But the tone of her voice wasn't quite what Howard had hoped for. He couldn't know that she was thinking of the last time she had picnicked in this area. Then it had been coke and sausage rolls—with Tim. They had joked and laughed and teased each other, and suddenly Julie felt an acute pang of guilt and almost of longing.

With a shock she realised that she had been far happier on that afternoon than she was at this moment.

The scooter buzzed along the coast road towards the Point, past the Nature Reserve, across the bridge over the river and taking the sharp left-hand bend in the road that now ran alongside the winding river. Above the river-bank were the tops of the masts of boats moored there. The road ended in a car park and gave way to the saltmarsh.

Today there was no sign of the coastguard's dark-blue-and-yellow land-rover. They left the scooter and walked towards a low dune about two hundred yards away. They dropped down into the sand, out of sight of anyone on the car park or on the river-bank. Vin tipped the three flares out on to the sand.

'Eh Vin, let me fire one today—please?'

'Well, I dunno. They're a bit dodgy.'

'Aw please, Vin. You've let 'em all off so far. Let me have a go.'

'All right then. I'll show you how to do it with this first one.' The flare began to smoke and the boy held it out in his right hand until it exploded and shot up into the air. Two pairs of eyes followed the line of the flare until it died and the red smoke drifted away.

'Now let me 'ave a go, Vin.'

'Wait a bit. Don't let's waste 'em. These are all we've got.'

'Oh come on—you're just trying to stop me 'aving a go.'

'No, I'm not.'

Mel made a grab for one of the flares. Her fingers closed round it and she twisted it out of Vin's hand. She pulled the cap from the base of the black canister and stripped the top off as she had seen Vin do. Then she struck the top with the cap. Immediately the flare ignited and began to smoke and splutter.

'Hold it away from you,' Vin shouted. 'It'll burn you.'

The magnesium began to boil out of the canister, a burning shower of red.

'Ouch!' Mel cried as it spat on to her hand and she flung the flare away from her, not looking where she threw it.

The flare hit the boy on the chest and exploded into his face.

Sea-birds rose from the ground in alarm as the marsh echoed with the sound of his screams.

Howard lay back, replete and content. It was sheltered and out of the wind it was

201

quite warm, drowsily warm. For a while they both dozed.

Whilst they slept the BBC weather forecast was broadcast at 13.55: '...*The area forecast for the next twenty-four hours...Tyne, Dogger, Fisher, German Bight, Humber... south-westerly five, increasing seven to gale eight, perhaps locally severe gale nine, then veering westerly and decreasing five. Heavy rain at times, then showers. Poor becoming moderate or good...*'

Out in the North Sea, Captain Karl Schlick heard the lunchtime BBC weather forecast for shipping.

He was making for the Lynn Well Lanby and from there through the Freeman Channel into the Deeps to be met by the pilot vessel in time to catch high water at 21.54 into the Port of St Botolphs. He had made this arrangement with the Port Authority twelve hours earlier over the radio.

So far it had been an uneventful trip and the medicinal bottle of rum had remained untouched in the locker on the bridge. But now, hearing the forecast, Schlick's hands gripped the wheel tighter, the sweat standing in beads on his forehead. He swore softly in his native German. That was the last thing he needed—bad weather. The pain gnawed at his gut and he shivered. He opened the locker, reached for the rum-bottle and took a gulp of the auburn liquid. This ship was a bastard to handle in rough seas with her fifteen-second roll, and more so than ever with the full cargo he was carrying of steel and paper and a deck cargo of packaged timber.

Schlick spoke through the intercom to his engineer. 'Ludendorff—I must have full speed.'

'That is suicide, Captain,' came back the swift retort from the engineer, an experienced man of twenty-five years at sea on all kinds of ships. A man who knew ships' engines, a man whose word should be heeded.

The pain stabbed again in his stomach as Schlick snapped back, 'We've got to make the Deeps or at least the Lynn Well. The weather is worsening rapidly. Full speed.'

'Full speed it is, Captain.' The engineer's clipped tone told Schlick that he was not pleased.

The Captain's mind was already troubled by the last interview he had had with his employers, the shipping company who owned the *Hroswitha*. When they had ordered him to take a cargo to Gothenburg and then bring this one from there across the North Sea to St Botolphs and another cargo back to his home port of Bremerhaven in West Germany, he had argued. 'The ship needs a refit. The engines have been causing trouble these last two trips.' He had thumped the agent's desk. 'She is not safe, like she is. And...'

He had been on the point of telling the man of his own problems, how his wife had begged him to see a doctor about these recurring stomach pains, but pride had prevented the words from being spoken.

Karl Schlick—a big and burly West German, disdainful of weakness—refused to admit to his ill-health. So many times he had brushed aside his wife's warning, promising her yet again, 'Next time, next time I am home.'

Now, here in the North Sea with the ship rolling and lurching beneath his feet, the pain in his inside stabbing incessantly and with the forecast of rough seas before he could make port, Captain Karl Schlick cursed himself heartily for his own stubbornness.

Julie awoke with a start and sat up. Something had disturbed her, but she was not sure what. She shivered and glanced at the sky. The sun had disappeared behind scudding black clouds and the breeze had strengthened to a north-westerly wind, cool and blustery.

She shook Howard. 'Howard—the weather's getting worse. We must get back.'

Howard sat up, yawned and stretched. Then he reached out for her and pulled her down on to the sand again. 'Now what's all the hurry?'

'Howard...'

His mouth silenced her, but a moment later he drew back from her, his eyes suddenly glinting with anger. 'You're a darned sight colder than your precious weather!'

He got up and began to gather their picnic things together.

Julie sat up again. 'I'm sorry, Howard. It's not that. But can't you see how the weather's changed even whilst we've been asleep?'

Howard gave a cursory glance towards the sky and then turned to look down on her. 'Look, Julie, I don't know if it's because your father's some kind of safety oracle around here or what, but you seem uncommonly panicky about the sea and the weather. Good God—it's only water for heaven's sake!'

Julie was scrambling to her feet, snatching up their gear. 'Don't let's waste time arguing. Will you just take my word for it that we should get back *now?*'

He raised his hands, palms towards her. 'Okay, okay, we'll go, we'll go.'

It was then that she heard the screaming.

Julie stood very still, her swift, anxious movements suspended by the eerie noise echoing across the marsh. 'What's that?'

Howard continued to gather their things, apparently unconcerned. 'What?'

'That noise. That screaming.'

Howard listened but only for a moment. 'A seagull, I should think.'

'That's no bird. That's someone—a person.' She ran quickly to the top of the dune behind which they had picnicked.

'Oh come on, Julie. I thought you were so anxious to be off.'

'There's someone over there. A girl running about.'

'Julie—it's nothing to do with us. It's a couple having a lark.'

But Julie would not be persuaded. 'No, she's in trouble, I'm sure of it.'

'It's none of our business. We don't want to get involved...'

Julie spun round. 'You may not want to, but I'm not going until I've found out what the matter is. We don't walk away from folks in trouble in *my* family!'

With that she flung down the napkin and cup she was holding and began to run towards the girl, whilst Howard carried on with the packing up of the picnic basket.

The young teenage girl, dressed in faded denims and an anorak, was running around without sense of purpose or direction, tears coursing down her face, her hands dragging at her long windblown hair.

Julie caught hold of her and shook her gently. 'What is it? What's the matter?'

The sobs increased. 'What *is* it?' Julie persisted.

The girl pointed with a trembling finger towards another sand-dune.

Julie let go of her and ran towards it and climbed it. She stood in shocked horror as she looked down at the ground beyond the sand-dune. A boy, possibly of a similar age to the girl, though Julie could not tell for she could not see his face, lay writhing on the ground, his hands covering his face. He was screaming and kicking and obviously in dreadful pain. Beside him lay the empty case of the used flare.

Fleetingly Julie thought that here must be the cause of all these hoax calls the lifeboat had been receiving, but there was no time to go into that now. Now the boy needed medical treatment—and fast!

Julie turned to the girl. 'Run—run to the shop on the Nature Reserve. Over the bridge and to the right.'

But the girl was beyond comprehension, she just ran around in circles, crying. She did not seem to take in what was being asked of her and Julie realised that the girl was hysterical.

Julie ran back to Howard, but he had gone from the sand-dune, the sand cleared of everything they had brought up from the boat. She ran to the river-bank and looked down to see Howard in the boat, calmly stowing away the picnic basket.

'Howard—there's a boy badly hurt over there. I'll run to the shop.' She nodded across the river to the Nature Reserve's Visitors' Centre which housed the Warden's bungalow, a shop and rooms for classes and courses. 'Can you go to him?

See if you can do anything?'

Howard looked up. 'Me? I'm no Florence Nightingale. What do you think I can do?'

For a moment Julie stood gaping at him, stunned by his callousness. 'Howard don't be so, so... Oh, I'm not wasting time arguing with you...' And she set off at top speed running up the road towards the bridge. Of course it might have been quicker, she reflected, to have gone across the river in the boat and up the other bank—the Centre was quite near that way. But with Howard in such an unhelpful mood...

As she ran her mind flickered from one thing to another: the lifeboat, the now injured boy who had most probably been the mysterious hoaxer, her father—even Tim—all this flashed through her mind in those few breathless moments. And Howard—gone in an instant was all the charm. What had, since the weekend began, been merely pinpricks of irritation camouflaged by his easy charm, had now been exposed in a moment of crisis revealing his arrogance, his pomposity, his selfishness—none of which had been noticeable in the very different atmosphere of University life.

His blatant refusal to help that poor boy had finally disgusted Julie.

Panting now with hard running, she crossed the bridge and ran along the road. The Nature Reserve Centre was still two or three hundred yards away. A car from the car park crossed the bridge behind her and slowed down beside her.

'Anything wrong, miss?' the driver shouted. Beside him, his wife craned forward, the two children stared at her from the rear window of the car.

'Yes, oh yes. Please could you give me a lift to the Centre, over there?' She pointed. 'There's been some sort of accident out there on the marsh. I must ring for an ambulance.'

'Oh blimey, get in quick, lass.'

The rear door of the car opened and Julie slid inside and leant back on the seat. Two pairs of huge brown eyes regarded her solemnly as she closed her eyes and took deep, shuddering breaths.

'What's happened? Someone belonging you hurt, is it?' the man's wife was asking.

Julie opened her eyes. 'No—no. I—we were picnicking and just packing up to go, when I heard this screaming. It looks as if a couple of youngsters—teenagers—have been playing with flares—you know, the sort a boat sets off if it's in trouble. And it looks as if one's gone off in the boy's face.'

The woman's hand flew to her mouth. 'Oh how dreadful!'

'Good God!' the driver muttered and drew to a halt outside the door of the shop. 'We'll wait for you, miss, whilst you ring up and then I'll come back with you.'

'Oh that is good of you.' Julie slipped from the car and dashed inside. Not everyone, then, she thought, was so unfeeling as Howard.

'Please,' she gasped to the woman behind the counter in the shop selling postcards, books, posters and souvenirs all about the natural environment and other items connected with the world of nature. 'Please could I phone for an ambulance? There's been an accident out on the marsh. A boy's badly hurt.'

'Oh dear. Yes, of course. In the office, here.' The woman opened a door behind her and Julie scurried around the counter.

With a trembling finger, she dialled nine-nine-nine.

'Emergency—which service?'

'Ambulance.'

'Connecting you. What number are you ringing from?'

Julie gave the operator the number and location. The ringing tone had scarcely sounded before a man's voice was answering, 'Ambulance Service.'

'This is Julie Macready. There has been an accident at Dolan's Point about two hundred yards from the bridge. A boy has been hurt in the face, I think by a flare. There's a girl with him. I don't think she's hurt, just dreadfully shocked.'

'Thank you, miss. Where are you phoning from?'

'The shop at the Nature Reserve Centre.'

'Can you wait there until the ambulance arrives, miss?'

'Yes, I'll go back to the bridge and wait there.'

'Right, miss. Thank you.'

The line went dead as the man rang off to take the necessary immediate action.

Julie breathed a sigh of relief, thanked the woman and went back outside. The family were still waiting in the car right outside the door.

'All right?' the man asked.

Julie nodded. Her knees were trembling now from the reaction. 'I've said I'll wait near the bridge until the ambulance comes.'

'Right, hop in. I'll drop you there and I'll go and see if I can do anything to help the lad. You can show me where he is. I belong to the St John's Ambulance Brigade at home.'

In a few minutes Julie was pointing out the figure of the girl still running about aimlessly near the dune behind which the injured boy lay.

'Right, you stay here, lass, and direct the ambulance when it gets here,' the man said.

Thankfully, Julie leant against the parapet of the bridge and watched the car swing round the sharp bend and speed back to the car park. She saw the man jump out and run across the marsh towards the girl and the sand-dune.

Julie glanced down river to where the *Nerissa* was still. She could see Howard sitting in the boat. He had not made any move to help in any way.

Julie felt almost sick with disgust—at Howard and at herself for having been so gullible as to be taken in by his smooth charm.

In only a few minutes she saw the

213

flashing light and heard the siren of the ambulance coming down the coast road. It slowed at the bridge and the nearside cab-door opened and she climbed inside, squashed in beside the driver and his mate.

'Hello, Julie. We wondered if it was you,' the driver said. She knew both the ambulance men, they had often been on hand after a lifeboat rescue.

'Where is this laddie, then?'

'Go right to the car park, Jim. And then he's about two hundred yards across the marsh, behind that sand-dune over there. Look, you can see a man standing on top of it waving. He stopped to help.'

The ambulance pulled into the car park. 'I don't reckon we can risk this on the marsh, do you, Chris?'

'No. We'll take the stretcher from here.'

Julie jogged at their side as they hurried across the flat marsh towards the sand-dune.

'Thank God you've come,' the car driver greeted them. 'He's in a hell of a mess. The thing must have exploded in his face. There's nothing I could do. I've nothing in my car to cope with that.'

'Best let the experts deal with it, sir,' said

one of the ambulance men, but without rancour. Obviously the man wanted to help.

'Oh I've some first-aid training but that's beyond my scope. I know when to let well alone. I've covered him up to try and keep him warm.'

'That's right.' Chris nodded approval but did not pause for an instant. The conversation was carried on all the while they were positioning the stretcher and bending over the boy.

'Where's the girl gone?' Julie asked suddenly.

'I saw her when I first got here,' the car driver said, 'but...' He glanced around him. 'I don't know where she is now.'

'Oh dear,' Julie said worriedly. 'She was in an awful state of shock.'

'Was she hurt?' said Jim as carefully they lifted the boy on to the stretcher. His screams had subsided now into a deep-throated continuous moan.

'No—at least, I don't think so. But she was hysterical with shock. We must find her.'

'Can you look for her, Julie, whilst we get this lad to the ambulance?'

'Of course.' She turned to the car driver.

'Will you look over there, inland? I'll go this way towards the sea. I know this marshy area pretty well.'

'Right you are.'

They separated to go in search of the girl.

Julie went as far as she could until the ground became soft and boggy and then turned towards the river and ran along the bank back towards where the *Nerissa* was moored.

Howard was standing on the bank above the boat. 'There you are. Are you ready *now...?*'

'No—the girl's missing. Have you seen her?'

'Girl? What girl?'

'The one who was crying so, she was in a terrible state.'

Howard cast his eyes heavenwards in exasperation and was about to say something when Julie heard a faint shout. It was the car driver searching in the opposite direction.

'Here—over here.'

She ran towards him.

'I've found her. She's here, behind this bush.'

The girl was huddled in a sorry, sobbing

heap, beating the sand with her fists and wailing.

'Look, the ambulance has gone with the lad. They said they'd either come back or radio for another. But I reckon it'd be quicker if I took her in my car to the local hospital, don't you? I know where it is.'

'All right. I'll phone the ambulance station and let them know what's happening.'

Together they helped the weeping girl, who allowed herself to be led, unresisting, towards the car.

'Thanks for all your help,' Julie said to the man and his family.

'Don't mention it. I always say you never know when you or yours might need a spot of help.' He jerked his head towards his own children sitting solemnly in the back of the car staring at the weeping girl beside them. 'I only hope there'd be someone there to help them if they ever need it. Cheerio, then.'

Julie raised her hand in farewell as the car moved off down the road, and she walked along the road and over the bridge back towards the Nature Reserve Centre to make another phone call.

Ten minutes later she rejoined Howard.

'Are you ready now?'

Julie glanced anxiously at the sky. 'Howard, I'm not sure we should even put to sea. It's...'

'Look, if you hadn't been so busy playing the Good Samaritan we could have been away ages ago. We're darned well going now!'

CHAPTER 14

The depression centred over the Midlands was moving rapidly towards the East coast. Between their afternoon scheduled programmes the BBC repeated the gale warnings:

'...*Tyne, Dogger, Fisher, German Bight, Humber...a warning of severe gales force nine, increasing storm force ten, imminent...*'

'Captain—Captain Schlick!' There was urgency and a tinge of fear in the First Mate's tone as he half-turned from the wheel.

'Ya, was ist denn, Droysen?' snapped Schlick, wiping his mouth with the back of his hand and recorking the bottle of rum. He was reaching towards the locker, the hiding-place, when the ship gave a violent lurch beneath his feet. The bottle slipped from his grasp and fell to the floor, shattering into a dozen pieces, the liquid spreading out across the wooden floor. The ship heaved again, but for a few seconds the Captain stood gazing down stupidly at the broken bottle and the rum—his one means of relief from this pain—dribbling about the floor.

'Captain—Ludendorff says the engines are over-heating. We must reduce to half-speed.'

'No,' Schlick bellowed. 'We've got to reach the shelter of the Wash before the storm breaks.'

The ship lurched and Droysen, his grip on the helm relaxing momentarily as he spoke to Schlick, found himself tossed backwards. The wheel spun freely.

Schlick lunged forward, his huge hands grasping the wheel. For a few moments he wrestled to bring the ship back to its original course, then he looked down at the man sprawling on the floor. 'Grosser Gott! Can't you handle a ship yet?' Schlick growled in his guttural German. 'You are not fit to be a first mate!'

Droysen, pale-faced, scrambled to his feet. His hand was bleeding where he had cut it on a piece of broken rum-bottle. He staggered towards the door, the ship heaving beneath his feet. He paused briefly in the doorway to glance back at Schlick. Who was he anyway to find fault? Droysen thought bitterly. A captain who drank on the bridge like he did was not fit to be a captain! Droysen weaved his way to his quarters to bandage his hand leaving Schlick to battle with the rolling ship.

Below in the engine room the engineer, Ludendorff, prowled about anxiously watching the over-worked engines as they grew hotter and hotter with every mile.

Away from the shelter of the Haven the sea was far rougher than even Julie had anticipated. There was no point now in arguing with Howard, all her concentration must be on crewing, on getting them back to shore.

She saw Howard mouthing words at her and though above the roar of the wind and the slap of the waves she could not hear what he said, by the look on his face she knew he was still ridiculing her anxiety. He looked as if he was enjoying the situation, the adventure, the challenge. He could see no danger.

They were still heading out to sea, running off the wind and Julie could feel the enormous strength of the wind, knew that the gusts would soon become too strong, too unexpected and sudden, for them to cope with.

She shouted above the howl of the wind and water and the flapping sails. 'Howard, *Howard*, tighten your sheets now. We're getting too far out.'

Howard, the helmsman, shrugged and grinned. 'Can't hear you, old thing,' he mouthed at her.

Julie gave an exaggerated grimace of fear, frowning and gritting her teeth at him and pointing northwards. But Howard only shook his head and laughed.

Julie inched her way the length of the boat to sit opposite him. Conversation was still difficult, she still had to yell and the wind caught at her words and whipped them away. 'Howard, we should go on to a reach. Look how choppy the water's getting out here and the wind...'

'Julie,' he said scornfully, 'I thought you were good at this sort of thing? You're chicken. I've told you I've done plenty of sailing in the Lakes...'

'What?' Julie shrieked. 'What did you say?'

'The Lakes—I've sailed a lot in the Lakes.'

'My God—the *Lakes*,' she whispered to herself, appalled. All that boasting, all that 'never out of my friend's boat' had that all been on the Lakes?

'Have you never sailed on the sea before?' she shouted at him now.

To her mounting horror, Howard shrugged and shook his head. He was saying something, trying to justify himself, but Julie was in no mood to listen. Anger, so alien to her gentle nature, welled up inside her. 'Howard, you're a fool if you don't take notice of me. I know this coast...'

Howard's expression darkened. 'Don't call *me* a fool, Julie. Nobody calls me a...'

The wind kicked against the dinghy, rocking it violently. Howard had allowed the boat to turn slightly to port so that a gust of wind was able to get behind the boom and flick it suddenly towards the helmsman's head.

'Look out!' Julie yelled. Howard ducked, only just in time and struggled to straighten the boat on course, with the wind dead astern once more. Julie went back to the jib.

Without giving the warning shout of 'stand by to gybe', Howard pulled in the main sheet and began to heel the boat to windward, crossing the boat as the boom came over. As the boat turned to port, the wind caught the mainsail fully, side on.

Suddenly Julie realised what was happening.

'Howard, Howard...' The wind savagely tore the words from her mouth as the boat went over to leeward. She saw Howard, arms and legs flailing briefly, fall backwards into the water. Only her own instinctive swift reaction prevented Julie from being tossed into the sea too. As the boat keeled over she scrambled up over the rising port gunwale and straddled the hull. Howard, floundering in the water, grabbed for the mast to save himself.

'No, not there, Howard, you'll pull her further under.' Julie yelled, but above the wind and the sea and the noise he could not hear her. She gesticulated wildly, but he did not see her. At that moment a wave buffeted against the boat, almost knocking Julie from her precarious perch and sweeping Howard further away from the boat.

At least it had stopped him causing a complete capsize, Julie thought as she tried to hook her foot on to the centreboard. Struggling against the heaving sea, she tried to grab the jibsheet on the slippery gunwale to get extra leverage, but frustratingly it flapped just out of reach. Desperately anxious to bring the boat upright before it turned turtle completely, she now manoeuvred herself so that one foot rested on the centreboard sticking out horizontally just above the surface of the water and keeping the other foot on the rubbing-strake and gripping the rubbing-strake with both hands. She leaned backwards carefully to lever the boat upwards, to lift the mast and drag the sails out of the water. Her arms felt as if they were being wrenched from their sockets, but grimly she hung on as she saw the mast begin to come clear of the water and she eased the pressure on the centreboard. Miraculously, it seemed to Julie in such seas, the boat came upright and with the agility born of danger, she clambered into the cockpit as the boat came up. The boat was still rocking dangerously, made more unstable now by the water it had shipped sloshing from side to side. Immediately Julie eased the mainsheet and the jibsheet until the sails flapped and then she began to bail out, all the time scanning the water around for sight of Howard. Only when she had the dinghy relatively safe could she start to look for him in earnest.

Then she saw his hands appear over the side of the boat and the craft rocked violently as Howard tried to haul himself into the boat.

Julie, scraping her knees, flung herself to the opposite side of the boat to balance him, but apparently he had not the fitness nor the strength to pull himself in. She saw his grip loosen and his fingers slither from sight. As the boat steadied she moved carefully across to peer over the side. Howard was still near the boat, his head bobbing up and down.

'The stern,' she yelled, completely out of patience now with his lack of what was to her elementary seamanship. 'Come in over the stern. I'll help you.'

Lying almost flat in the boat but leaning out over the stern, Julie guided Howard.

'Grab the transom.'

'What?'

'This,' she snapped and slapped it with her fist and muttered, 'God, don't you know anything?' Then louder she shouted at him. 'Take a deep breath and push yourself down in the water first and then pull up as hard as you possibly can. Don't let go of this, though.'

To his credit, Howard now did as he was told, but it took three attempts plus Julie grabbing hold of him and hauling him in, before he landed, a gasping, shuddering heap in the bottom of the boat.

Julie now took charge. She gave Howard a few moments to rest and then she started issuing orders. 'The quicker we make land the better,' she yelled grimly into his ear. 'Haul in the mainsheet, get back to the tiller and let's get moving! This wind's getting worse by the minute.'

Stiffly Howard crawled aft and took hold of the tiller. Gone was all his conceit, all his arrogance, washed away in those terrifying moments in the raging sea.

'Get that sheet in!' Julie shouted again.

With numb fingers Howard obeyed her command.

Satisfied that he was at least doing

what she told him now, Julie turned her attention to the worsening weather. In these conditions it would be sufficient to use just the mainsail, no point in causing themselves more difficulty. As long as they reached the shore safely it didn't matter if it took them a bit longer.

Or did it?

She looked up at the scudding clouds above them, the darkening world around them and the rising, bucking seas beneath them.

If only, Julie thought in a rush of emotion, it were the reassuring figure of Tim in the boat with her, with his expertise, his knowledge and, yes, his love for her, instead of this conceited oaf who had put them in such danger. How could Julie ever forgive herself and now she realised just what it must have cost her father, too, to have remained silent, for she knew he must have seen through Howard Marshall-Smythe from the start.

And what must he be feeling now, that father of hers? Was he aware of the danger she was in? His face was floating before her mind's eye all the while her numb fingers worked at the sheets. Unbidden, beside the face of her father, she saw Tim, saw the hurt, the anxiety, and knew in an instant how she had wounded him too.

If only we get back, she prayed silently. If only...

Then she knew what she should do. Fire a flare. Her faith was such that she knew that was all she had to do.

Fire a red distress flare and the lifeboat—and her father—would come.

She scrambled towards the locker under the foredeck and felt for the package of hand-held flares. There were no flares in the place where they should be.

'Howard. Howard!' She crawled back towards him. 'The flares—the red flares. Where are they?'

'I don't know. I just asked the chap at the shop to fit her out. I suppose he put them somewhere.'

There was nowhere else they could be except where she had already looked. Julie's heart pounded. She swallowed to try to ease the tightening feeling of panic in her throat.

There were no distress flares aboard the *Nerissa*.

For a time she still thought they could make it.

They were sailing a broad reach north-wards parallel to the shore, as they had earlier in the day, but now the conditions were very different. The sea was a cold, inhospitable fury, the wind, though predominantly still from the south-west, was gusting in all directions and at times the gusts reached storm force.

With an inexperienced helmsman and a young girl, who, though her knowledge of the sea was sound, had not the physical strength against such conditions, disaster was inevitable.

It came when they tried to tack into the wind, to begin beating towards the shore and safety.

She felt the boat begin to rock dangerously and glanced behind her. Howard, his hands still clutching the mainsheet and the tiller, was rocking backwards and forwards, his mouth open, his eyes glazed with fear.

Julie scrambled to the stern and peered over.

The rudder blade had risen up out of position. Obviously Howard had not set the tension on the downhall correctly—the cord was jammed under the water. She grabbed at the hook and tried to stretch it forward but the rubber cord was held fast. Obviously, in the rough seas they were now encountering, the rudder stock had been badly damaged all because of Howard's negligence.

But was it negligence, Julie thought in that awful moment, or just sheer ignorance?

For the first time in her young life, Julie Macready felt very frightened of the ocean.

The *Nerissa* was careering madly out of control. Julie made a desperate effort to save the boat, but Howard, petrified, seemed unable to move.

The dinghy tipped sideways, the starboard gunwale almost dipping beneath the waves. Julie turned to try and grab hold of Howard as he was falling backwards again into the water, his shriek of pure terror echoing in her ears. The boat rocked this way and that, shipping water, the mainsail swung dangerously and Julie turned in time to see Howard throw up his hands in fear, releasing the tiller and the mainsheet in one instant. The boom swung loose. Julie saw it coming and instinctively ducked down, yelling as she did so and trying to pull Howard down with her. But he took the full force of the blow on his shoulders knocking him head first over the stern into the water.

Julie caught hold of the snaking sheet, but the boat was rocking so violently and shipping water, and a huge wave finished the job.

The boat keeled over and Julie felt herself falling into the sea.

She surfaced about two yards from the boat and struck out strongly for it. The sea was churning and tossing the sailing dinghy, but, fiercely determined, Julie clambered up on to the boat which was fortunately still only on its side. Again she tried to right the craft, but Howard, now panic-stricken, was clinging to the mast, forcing it below the level of the water, tipping the boat more and more towards a complete capsize. Julie yelled at him, pointing to the mast to try to indicate that he should release his hold on it. For a moment she thought he had understood. Then to her horror she saw him grasp the mast and fling it upwards out of the water. The sails came free of the water almost like a rubber suction disc giving way, catapulting the boat upright, but too far, for it rolled right over, thrusting

Julie down into the water again and this time the dinghy turned right over into a complete capsize.

Julie, caught unawares, floundered in the sea for a few moments, trying to catch her breath, trying to regain her self-control. Again she fought her way to the boat and now there was no hope of righting it again. Aiming for the leeside, she felt around under the upturned craft until her fingers closed on a loose sheet. Keeping fast hold of this, she manoeuvred herself around the end of the boat looking for Howard.

There was no sign of him.

Her legs were beginning to go numb— the water was terribly cold and so choppy. Julie realised her only chance of survival was to climb up on to the hull of the boat. Almost exhausted, and already weakened by her strenuous efforts to keep the boat afloat each time it had capsized, three times she tried to scrabble her way up the slippery upturned hull.

At the fourth attempt buoyed up by a wave she found herself sprawling across the fibre-glass hull, but with sadistic cruelty where one wave had helped her a moment ago, the next, bigger than the last, struck the boat and the girl.

She felt herself being washed off, with no hand-hold on the smooth surface, helpless against the power of the sea, tossed and engulfed like a piece of flotsam.

The waves closed over her head.

CHAPTER 15

The wind howled over the *Hroswitha*, tugged at the tarpaulins covering the deck cargo and stretched the ropes that tied them down. The ship ploughed on, the ropes strained even more with every roll.

The intercom buzzed on the bridge. 'Captain,' came Ludendorff's gruff voice. 'The engines are overheating—the starboard one has seized up completely.'

Schlick swore volubly. 'Can't you do your job? You're the engineer, aren't you?'

The engineer's voice came loudly into the wheelhouse. 'Can't you captain a ship, you drunken fool?'

Droysen appeared in the doorway in time to hear the engineer's words, distorted by the communicating system but their meaning clear even above the howl of the wind and the storm. Words that echoed the First Mate's own feelings.

Then Droysen saw Schlick's fingers slacken on the wheel, watched horror-stricken as the big man's legs buckled beneath him and he crumpled to the floor. The wheel swung wildly to and fro and the ship pitched out of control in the heavy seas. Droysen made a dive for the wheel, but Schlick, rolling in agony on the floor and clutching his gut, got in the way and brought Droysen down too. The two men sprawled on the floor, Droysen half on top of the older man.

The First Mate dragged himself up and managed to put the ship on to automatic pilot. That at least would give him time to radio for help.

'Mayday, Mayday,' he spluttered into the microphone. '*Hroswitha* calling St Botolphs Port. Mayday, Mayday!' His voice rose in panic whilst behind him, Captain Schlick tried to haul himself upright. The pain in his gut was terrible—the worst he had ever known it—and he thought he could taste blood rising in his throat. He clawed his way across the heaving floor and grabbed the mike from Droysen.

'Let me. Find the deckies. See—Luden-dorff.'

Droysen's eyes looked huge in his white, pinched face. He licked his lips, blinked several times and seemed to take a grasp of his rising panic. He staggered out into the howling gale.

Schlick called up the agents in the Port of St Botolphs and also the Harbour Master giving the ship's position and informing them that one engine had failed and the other was severely overheating. But he could not be sure whether he had been heard—there was no response from anyone—just a mass of crackling over the receiver.

For all Schlick knew he was broadcasting into empty airwaves.

Schlick felt the pain squeezing, stabbing, twisting his guts. The bile rose in his throat as his ship lurched beneath him at the mercy of the North Sea.

Schlick was slumped in the seat near the radio, the mike grasped in his left hand whilst his right he kept pressed into his stomach. If only he had not dropped that blasted bottle! His face was grey and despite the cold wind yowling around the bridge, beads of sweat stood out on his forehead.

He had sent Droysen in search of the deckhands, the three Turkish seamen who had apparently disappeared below decks the minute the weather had worsened. Droysen stumbled in, his face and shoulders were saturated from the flying spray, his hat had gone, torn off by the whipping wind.

'They're useless—those deckhands! One's okay, he's gone to check the cargo, but the other two are cowering below like a couple of gibbering idiots!' the First Mate reported.

'You're not much better yourself,' Schlick muttered and winced as the pain stabbed once more.

'I'd have no fear if I had faith in my Captain. I'm not used to shipping with a drunkard.' It was a statement the quiet Droysen had never expected to hear himself make. Appalled at his own daring, he waited for Schlick's rage to explode. For a moment, anger gave Schlick's face a tinge of colour, then he groaned as the pain twisted again and thrust thick vomit into his throat.

'I'm—I'm not drunk. But I will admit—

236

to being a fool! I'm—sick—sick. This pain—I've had it weeks—months and I ignored it—refused to believe I—could be ill. Now I am being made to pay.'

Droysen stared at him and slowly he realised the truth. Captain Schlick was no alcoholic—he had scarcely touched the bottle in his locker during the early, smooth part of the passage. Droysen now understood. It was only when the weather got rough and the engines started overheating that he had seen Schlick reaching into the locker again and again.

'Captain.' Droysen was hesitant again now, his moment of rebellion over. 'I don't know if I should—if you should—it may do more harm—but I have a bottle of brandy in my...'

'Get it, man, get it,' Schlick almost implored, stretching out shaking fingers towards the First Mate. Droysen was still staring at the sick man. How clear it was now. How could he not have seen it before? He stepped backwards and then hurried out.

Whilst he waited, Schlick once more broadcast his mayday message and prayed that Droysen would not drop the bottle on his way back.

Someone stepped into the wheelhouse. It was not Droysen but one of the Turkish seamen.

'Captain—rope on deck cargo. She go...' He made a clicking noise with his mouth and flung his hands wide apart.

'Broken, you mean?'

The man nodded. 'Broken—yes.'

Droysen appeared in the doorway behind the seaman, the bottle of brandy in his hands. Schlick's eyes were on the bottle, his hand reaching out towards it. For a brief moment Droysen still hesitated, unsure whether the sick man should really take more alcohol. But the pleading in the big man's eyes was more than he could stand. He handed the brandy to Schlick, who opened it with trembling fingers and drank deeply. He closed his eyes and then let out a great sigh.

Whether the brandy actually helped so swiftly or whether it was merely the man's belief that the pain would now ease, when Schlick opened his eyes again, he was already once more alert and able to think rationally again.

'Droysen—I can manage now. Go and inspect the deck cargo. This deckie says a rope's snapped. And get him'—Schlick nodded towards the Turk—'to fire a red flare.'

'Right, Cap'n.' Droysen disappeared. The Turk followed, but not before he had cast a sly look at the brandy-bottle.

Moments later, through the driving rain, Schlick saw Droysen inching his way along the starboard rail. The howling gale was whipping up the water and twenty-five-foot waves were coming at them now. Behind him on the poop, the Turk fought to keep his balance on the slippery deck whilst he detonated a parachute flare. The first shot up into the air, but the wind extinguished it. The second flared briefly, shot over the deck rail and immediately fell into the water. At the third attempt the deckie failed to hold it properly and the rocket ricocheted off the superstructure, fell on to the deck and fizzled out. Muttering Turkish oaths, he made a fourth attempt and this time the red flare snaked up into the sky and burst and the tiny white parachute opened. The gale tore at it relentlessly, but the flare glowed red in the lowering sky.

Schlick saw the flare go up. Even if his radio message had not got through, perhaps someone would see the flare. He

239

glanced down at his instruments. In a few minutes he would be well within the boundaries of the Wash. He prayed that that would give them more shelter, but then, he realised, there were the sandbanks on either side. With this weather and the ship in this condition, those banks could prove a hazard rather than a haven. Somewhere far beneath his feet he felt a shudder pass through the hull of his ship and then there was only the sound of the sea and the wind and rain.

For some reason the second engine had stopped. Now the *Hroswitha* was drifting helplessly.

Schlick squinted through the screen. Through the slanting rain and the turbulent sea, he could just see—intermittently—the fitful light on the Lynn Well Lanby, the buoy shaped like an upturned mushroom.

Wincing again as the pain stabbed afresh, Schlick operated the anchor mechanism and let out a sigh of relief as the anchor bit and for a while the ship was held, tossed and buffeted by the gale and the huge waves, but reasonably safe for the time being.

But for how long?

Pete Donaldson awoke to find the place beside him in the big bed empty. He had returned home the previous evening to an empty house. He had showered and made a plate of sandwiches ready for Angie's coming home and then he had sat with his feet up in front of the television. He had awoken to find Angie shaking his shoulder. 'Hey—you should be in bed, love, if you're that tired.'

Pete yawned and stretched. 'What time is it?'

'Half-ten. You go up. I'll have a quick shower.'

Pete had dragged himself up the stairs, his eyes almost closing, his limbs heavy with tiredness. He had tried to stay awake, had heard the shower running and Angie singing to herself...

When Angie came into the bedroom, her cheeks pink and glowing from the shower, her hair damp and curling, Pete was gently snoring.

And now, this morning, he had still been asleep when she had slipped out of bed and gone to help at the café again.

'Well,' said Pete aloud to the otherwise empty house. 'I'm not staying here on my own all day. I'll go to the café

241

for my dinner. I'll get to see my wife somehow!' He grinned, ruefully amused at how Fate seemed to be conspiring to keep himself and his lovely Angie apart this weekend.

The café was absolutely packed with mackintosh-clad and bedraggled holiday-makers. There was even a queue forming near the cash desk waiting for a table to become vacant. Pete threaded his way through the throng towards the kitchens. As he approached the swing door, a pink-faced Angie came through from the kitchen, her blonde hair dishevelled, a harassed frown on her smooth forehead and balancing two dishes of soup on each hand.

'Oh—hello, darling.'

'Hello, love. You look a bit busy.'

She smiled, the corners of her mouth turning down in mock annoyance. 'Just a bit! It's the weather, I suppose.'

Pete side-stepped to let her pass. 'Any dinner going for a hungry husband?'

'We're about to stop serving dinners now, but see Mum in the kitchen, love,' Angie replied over her shoulder. 'I'll be back in a mo.'

As he went through the swing door, the

heat from the kitchen hit him like a solid wave. 'Phew!' he said to his mother-in-law, an attractive, plump blonde—an older edition of Angie, 'how on earth do you stand this all day?'

'I sometimes wonder, lad. Want some dinner? Help yourself.'

'Thanks, Peg.' Anything but her Christian name did not suit the young, energetic forty-five-year-old woman. Only Angie ever called her 'Mum.'

Pete piled his plate high with steak-and-kidney pie, mashed potatoes and peas and was just sitting down in a comparatively quiet corner of the busy kitchen to enjoy his lunch when above the clatter of pans and the bubbling saucepans he heard the familiar bang of the lifeboat maroon.

Angie came through the swing door just in time to see Pete heading for the back door out into the yard. 'See you, Peg,' he was shouting to her mother. 'Tell Angie...' But he never looked back to see his wife standing there.

The telephone call had come through to the coastguard just before three o'clock. The voice said, 'I reckon I've just seen a red flare go up somewhere out in the

Wash. I'm sorry I can't be any more precise than that.'

'May I have your name, sir?' Jack Hansard asked the caller.

'My name—well, yes,—but does that matter?'

'Just to make it official, sir.'

'Oh yes, of course. Raymond Graham.'

'Where exactly were you when you saw the flare?'

'I was out on the mud flats south of the Haven—doing a spot of bird-watching, but it got so rough, I decided to pack it in. I was just getting all my gear together and I happened to glance out to sea and I saw this thing—well, it looked like a flare. I mean, I can't be absolutely definite, but I thought I ought to report it anyway.'

'Quite right, sir. Can you give me any sort of direction?'

'Oh dear,' said the voice over the telephone, wavering a little now. 'I'm not very good at guessing directions. Sort of in the mouth of the Wash, I'd say.'

'Right, sir. Where are you ringing from?'

'The Visitors' Centre at the Nature Reserve.'

'Would you be good enough to wait there for about ten minutes and I'll come

244

down? If you could show me where you were when you saw the signal, it would give me a much better idea and be a great help.'

'Yes, of course I'll wait.'

'Thank you very much, sir.'

The call completed, Jack Hansard dialled the boathouse number.

'Macready.'

'Iain—I'm not sure, but we may have had our friend the hoaxer on the line again.'

Macready swore softly under his breath but listened intently whilst the coastguard continued. 'Mind you, it is a bit different this time—he did give his name.' Swiftly Jack Hansard repeated all the information the caller had given him.

'Mmmm—well, we can't ignore it, that's certain. Have you checked with St Botolphs?'

'Not yet, but I will.'

'I'll get on to Bill and we'll probably get the lads on standby.'

'Right, Iain. I'll come back to you in a few minutes.'

Ten minutes later they were once again on the line to each other exchanging news.

Jack reported, 'The Harbour Master reports that they've no vessels overdue, but there's one—a German coaster out of Gothenburg—the *Hroswitha*—expected on tonight's high water which has failed to report in recently. The last they heard was the ETA over fourteen hours ago. Since then, nothing. The Harbour Master's office have tried to raise her, but so far without success.'

'It could be her in trouble then,' Macready murmured. 'Bill has approved a launch and we're calling in the lads between us.'

'I'm just off to the Point. The phone caller is supposed to be waiting at the Visitors' Centre. I'll radio you from there.'

As Macready turned from the phone he found Tim hovering at his elbow. 'Away and fire two maroons, Tim.'

'Right, Mr Macready.'

'And Tim...'

The youth paused. 'Yes?'

'You're in the crew, son.'

For a fleeting moment before he ran to detonate the maroons, Tim's face was a picture of joy, the culmination of all his years of devotion.

He was to take part in a real service.

'Thanks, Mr Macready. *Thanks!*'

Then he was off at a gallop across the road, down the bank and over the grass to the circular stone from where the maroons were fired. Seconds later the rocket shot up into the scudding sky and burst in a shower of green sparks. The high wind whipped them away and tossed them out to sea. A second rocket followed, but the signal was not so clear amidst the roar of the gale.

The centre of the depression which had begun its journey hundreds of miles away in the Atlantic now lay directly over the Saltershaven stretch of coastline.

CHAPTER 16

As the lifeboat procession crossed the sand, Macready, his mouth tight, glanced at the sky. It was going to be very rough out at sea, he knew. The forecast had been bad enough and his own intuition feared even worse.

'Mr Macready, Mr Macready,' a breathless voice hailed him and he turned to see

Sandy running across the beach.

Macready stepped to one side to allow the lifeboat to continue its progress towards the sea. 'What is it?'

Panting, Sandy said, 'Your Julie—and her friend—they're out in a day-boat. Thought you should know.' He nodded towards the sky, as knowledgeable in his way as Macready, as all these men who worked the sea. 'Reckon we're in for a real blow.'

'Aye,' Macready said shortly. 'Thanks, Sandy. Would ya tell Jack Hansard for me. We're away on a service. A red flare has been sighted out in the Wash. We think it could be a coaster on its way to St Botolphs. If ye'd tell Jack and Bill Luthwaite, too, they'll—they'll keep an eye out.' There was an unusual catch in Macready's voice.

Never before had his own daughter been in trouble out at sea, needing his help perhaps. And now he was going several miles away to the aid of a foreign ship.

Unless, of course, this call was yet another cruel hoax.

On their way out to sea, Macready scanned the surface. There was nothing. No sign of a small craft. The wind was strengthening by the minute almost and the conditions at sea approximated to Force Ten on the Beaufort Scale with a wind speed in excess of fifty knots and waves in the open sea of over thirty feet from trough to overhanging crest.

Grim-faced Macready set a course towards the mouth of the Wash, every moment taking him further away from the area where Julie might be.

Jack Hansard entered the shop at the Visitors' Centre and approached a man leaning against the counter talking to the woman behind it.

'I'm looking for a Mr Raymond Graham.'

The man straightened up. 'That's me.'

'Ah!' There was satisfaction in the coastguard's voice and he smiled at the stranger. 'You don't know how relieved I am to see you waiting here, sir. We've launched the lifeboat on the strength of your call...'

For a moment the man looked worried. 'Oh dear. I only hope I'm right.'

Jack Hansard reassured him. 'No matter, sir, as long as you *genuinely* thought you saw something unusual out there, then we must take action. The snag is, you see, we've been having several hoax calls and from this area, and when your call came through—' Jack spread his hands—'well, we just couldn't be sure, you see...'

The man's expression lightened. 'Oh I understand...'

'Excuse me,' the woman said, a little hesitantly. 'But I couldn't help overhearing. We had something happen here about two hours ago. A girl came rushing in here and phoned for the ambulance. She'd found a young lad on the marsh—just over the river—badly burned in the face. She reckoned him and a girl with him had been setting off flares.'

'Really?' Jack was interested immediately. 'Was it the girl with the boy who phoned?'

'No—oh no, it was Mr Macready's daughter who telephoned.'

'Julie? Julie Macready?'

'That's right.'

'Thanks very much, love.' He turned back to the man. 'Let's go and take a look.'

Outside they climbed into the coastguard's landrover and Jack Hansard drove on to the bridge. Here he paused and glanced to right and left briefly, up and down river, hoping to see a sailing-dinghy that could be the one belonging to Julie Macready's friend, moored in the shelter of the River Dolan.

Several boats were moored there, but Jack knew this district well enough to recognise most of them as permanent moorings. Although he had not actually seen the boat he was now looking for, he knew roughly what to look for.

There was no sign of an unfamiliar day-boat of the right size anywhere along the river-bank.

He sighed inwardly. He had so hoped to be able to report back to a worried Macready that his daughter was safely sheltering down at the Haven.

Now he could not do so.

Surely they had not put out to sea again. Julie knew better than to do that in this weather.

'I was over there—just near the mouth of the river,' the man, Raymond Graham, was saying. 'And I saw a funny sort of light go up over there.' He was pointing in the direction, Jack knew, of the Lynn Well Lanby.

'Thank you, sir. You've been a great help.'

251

'Well—I do hope so. Is that all?'

'I think so, sir. Do you want a lift back to town?'

'No, it's quite all right, thanks, my car's here—on the car park.'

'Right you are then, sir,' Jack said as the man got out of the cab. 'Many thanks.'

Jack Hansard turned the landrover and went along the river bank. He would just take one more look for Julie before he radioed Macready.

Out at sea, the going was very rough. Pete responded as a call came in from the coastguard.

'...Reference sighting of red flares. This looks like a genuine distress signal. The caller was waiting at the Point and according to information he gave me, the signal appeared to be in the area of the Lynn Well Lanby.'

Pete made the usual reply and added, '...We are on course for the Lanby. Over.'

But Jack still had something else he must say and at his next words Pete turned towards his coxswain. 'Jack must want a link call, Mac. He's asking for channel six.'

When all rescue broadcasting was carried

out on channel sixteen, the request by the coastguard for channel six meant only one thing—he wanted a personal word with Macready.

'Take over, will you, Fred, for a moment.' He handed over the wheel to his second coxswain and took the phone from Pete.

'Hello, Jack. Iain here.'

'Iain—there's something you should know.' Now Jack Hansard was speaking not as coastguard but to his friend, Iain Macready.

'It seems as if the hoaxer may have been caught. About two hours ago an accident occurred on the marsh. A boy burnt in the face setting off a flare. And the call for the ambulance was made by your Julie. They must have put into the Haven and seen the accident. But, Iain, I'm sorry, the boat's not here now. I've had a real good look around. They must have put back out to sea. In view of the weather conditions, I'm going to report it officially. I'm so sorry...'

'Thanks, Jack.'

Silently Macready handed the radio/telephone back to Pete and took the wheel from Fred Douglas.

Macready glanced at Tim. For a moment he thought the boy was about to be sea-sick. Tim's face was surf-white. Tim—sea-sick? Impossible! Then the older man realised.

Tim had overheard the message from the coastguard and now he too knew that Julie Macready was perhaps somewhere out here in these swelling seas.

With the crack of a pistol shot another wire rope snapped and with a rumble that reverberated through the hull of the ship, a section of the deck cargo shifted and the coaster began to list to starboard. For a while the anchor held but as the weather deteriorated and the seas grew stronger with waves of twenty-five to thirty feet, the anchor could no longer hold the fully-laden coaster and, dragging her cable and now listing heavily to starboard, the *Hroswitha* lurched nearer and nearer to the sandbanks on the eastern coast of the Wash.

Droysen hacked at the ropes holding the section of packaged timber where two had already broken. Schlick had given him the order to let that section causing the trouble go overboard. The ship tossed about on the ocean like a cork, the seas washing constantly across the deck. Droysen paused, breathing hard and tried again. One rope gave and the package began to slide towards him. He stumbled backwards as the timber slithered into the sea. The boat pitched momentarily upright with the relief of some of the imbalance of weight, but there were still several packages left that needed to be ditched. Once again the ship settled back to her starboard list.

Schlick watched from the bridge as Droysen struggled forward again and raised his axe.

The deckhand who had fired the flares sidled into the bridge room. Schlick turned and barked an order, gesticulating towards the cargo deck. 'Go and help the First Mate with the cargo.'

The deckie looked through the rain-washed screen and fear crossed his face. He shook his head. 'No—no—I...'

'Get down there,' Schlick roared and made as if to lunge towards the Turk. The deckie went.

Schlick watched as the deckhand made his way gingerly along the starboard side of the sloping deck, hanging on to the ropes holding the cargo, towards where Droysen was still hacking away with the axe. At the moment when the deckhand was almost up to the First Mate, the axe chopped the remaining strand of rope and another huge pack began to move towards the edge. The Turk—without the sense to keep out of the way until Droysen had completed his job and caught sight of him—had been trying to cross directly in front of the very pack of cargo Droysen was attempting to release. As the tightly packed timber moved, the deckie squealed as it lumbered towards him, catching him a glancing blow on the arm and—luckily for him—knocking him to one side on to the deck. It could so easily have carried him overboard with it as it plunged into the water. The ship rolled again and Droysen struggled towards the deckhand. The sea washed over the side, the waves running across the deck, slapping against the remaining packages and then receding, falling back into the sea and threatening to carry the Turk with them. Droysen made a grab at the man and dragged him away from the edge and towards the shelter of the superstructure and then up to the bridge.

If the deckhand had been wet before, he was now absolutely saturated. He was gibbering wildly in his native tongue and clutching his arm. Blood oozed from the wound and ran through his fingers.

'What the hell...?' Schlick turned as Droysen and the deckhand lurched in through the doorway.

'Give him a swallow of that brandy, Captain,' Droysen requested.

Schlick glanced at the wound on the man's arm. He could see the injury was serious—the man must obviously be in considerable pain. The Turk continued to jabber. As if in protest against the precious liquid's being given away, the pain in Schlick's stomach stabbed relentlessly.

'Very well—but only a little.'

Droysen sat the deckhand in the chair near the radio, opened the locker and brought out the bottle and gave it to the Turk who uncorked it and raised it to his lips.

'I must get back to the cargo deck,' Droysen muttered and once more disappeared out into the storm.

Gulp after gulp of the brandy was disappearing until Schlick shouted, 'That's enough.' But still the deckhand continued to pour the spirit down his throat until incensed, his own pain almost forcing him to double up, Schlick lunged towards the Turk, his huge hands outstretched to grasp the brandy.

A brawl followed, with both men's hands clamped on the bottle, swaying together, flung from one side of the bridge to the other, they were locked in a macabre dance, whilst the ship heaved and plunged. Out on the wave-lashed, windswept deck, Droysen was flung against the timber and then back again to the deck rail. Clinging to the handrail he glanced towards the bridge, but through the rain he could see nothing. Huge waves were coming at them now and the ship was turning abeam to the waves, in danger of being bowled over by the next wave. Droysen, soaked and gasping for breath, grappled his way back towards the bridge and hauled himself up the ladder. He arrived in time to see the Captain wrestling with the Turk, the bottle of brandy between them.

A thirty-foot wave struck the ship side on and she rolled even further over to starboard, the deckrail almost dipping momentarily beneath the waves. Schlick and the Turk were flung to one corner, the bottle crushed between them. Droysen felt himself slithering across the floor. For what seemed an eternity—though in fact it was only a few seconds—the whole world seemed one of confusion—of flailing arms and legs, of roaring seas and lashing rain and howling wind and the noise of the ship creaking and groaning under immense stress.

This is it, Droysen thought, amazingly clear-headed. The ship is going to capsize and go down.

But with a miraculous instinct for survival, the *Hroswitha* rolled upright again, the heavy cargo in her hold giving ballast to the stricken vessel.

Droysen scrambled up. Over his shoulder he looked down at the two men extricating themselves from the corner. The bottle had smashed into four pieces. Schlick's hand was bleeding and the Turk's cheek as well as his injured arm now oozed blood. Schlick swore in guttural German but the oath ended in a grimace of pain and he clutched his stomach and rolled backwards and forwards on the floor. The Turk eyed Droysen warily.

'You—out!' Droysen commanded shortly, the pale grey eyes in his pale-skinned face glittering menacingly. In contrast the swarthy Turk slunk away, still half-crouching and making a great play of his injured arm.

Droysen glanced down cynically at his Captain, marvelling that when he had first come aboard the *Hroswitha* he had feared this man who now brawled with a deckhand over a bottle of brandy and rolled about on the floor of his bridge.

Droysen squinted through the glass screen of the wheelhouse. The anchor was no longer holding them, they were being dragged relentlessly by the wind and the heavy seas towards the sandbank known as Middle Bank off the north-west coast of Norfolk.

Then, through the murk, Droysen thought he saw a boat to starboard—a lifeboat, but then it plunged from view and he thought he had wishfully imagined it, his eyes playing cruel tricks.

Then, as the *Hroswitha* was borne aloft on a wave, he saw below in the trough, the lifeboat battling its way towards them. If he had had the strength left, Droysen would have cheered. As it was all he could do was to cling on and wait. Only moments before he had been sure he faced death, now as the courageous lifeboat approached, he was just as certain that now he would be saved.

At the same moment that Droysen first spotted the rescue boat, aboard the *Mary Martha Clamp* Chas Blake in the bows glimpsed the coaster.

Macready sent a radio message to Jack Hansard in his landrover on the seafront at Saltershaven and to Breymouth, asking them to relay a message to the Harbour Master at St Botolphs that a coaster obviously making for his port was in distress near the Lynn Well Lanby. The westerly wind and the tidal flow were driving the helpless vessel, bows foremost, towards a sandbank off the Norfolk coast known as Middle Bank.

Macready took the lifeboat around the stern of the coaster and approached it cautiously on the starboard side. The coaster was listing heavily towards them and the only way to get the crew off would be for Macready to put his lifeboat alongside almost directly under the heaving, tilting ship. He could see that part of the deck cargo had already gone and that the remaining packages had shifted and were straining at the ropes.

The loose tarpaulin flapped about on the deck and ropes snarled and snaked in the gale-force winds.

He could see no one on the ship. The loudhailer in these conditions was useless. If radio contact was also impossible, it would have to be morse signalling.

'See if you can raise anyone on her, Pete,' Macready said. Already his crew were taking up their stations and securing themselves to the lifeboat by clipping a line on to the deck rail.

Pete made the call but when he flicked the switch only crackling and interference filled the cockpit of the lifeboat. He tried again and this time, amidst all the noise came a faint reply in English but with a distinctly German accent.

'Lifeboat, lifeboat, this is the *Hroswitha*. Engines—out of action. Captain...' There then followed a blur of words and the final word... 'injured.'

'What was that?' Macready asked.

Pete spoke into the phone. '*Hroswitha*, this is Saltershaven lifeboat. Say again, please. Over.'

'...Captain—sick. One deckhand—injured.'

Macready's face was grim. 'Can they receive a breeches-buoy?'

The reply came back that there was only himself—the First Mate—to receive it. He had no idea where the three deckhands and cook were. Nor could he raise a reply from the engine-room. As the message came piece by piece into the lifeboat's cockpit, Macready saw four figures appear on the deck of the coaster, clinging to the superstructure and attempting to make their way to the starboard side of the ship nearest to the lifeboat.

'Four of his crew seem to be looking after number one,' Macready murmured. Then aloud he said to Pete, 'Ask him if the Captain can walk.'

Pete relayed the question and Droysen hesitated and then replied negatively.

Macready again shouted to Pete above the howl of the wind and the sea. 'Ask Breymouth if we can have the helicopter.'

The lifeboat's responsibility was the saving of life and the coxswain's one aim was to get the injured and sick members of the crew off the coaster and to hospital as quickly as possible. If he could get the crew aboard the lifeboat and then the helicopter could air-lift the sick captain and the injured deckhand, they would reach hospital so much quicker than if he had to take them all the way back to Saltershaven.

Pete Donaldson requested Breymouth for the assistance of the Sea King helicopter, but their immediate reply was that it was already out assisting another lifeboat off the east coast of Norfolk on a service.

'We're on our own, then,' Macready murmured as he received the news. 'Right—we're going in!'

Grim-faced, the lifeboat coxswain inched nearer and nearer, desperately trying to control the bucking Oakley and bring her close to the stricken vessel.

Above the upturned faces of the lifeboat-men, the ship's four crew members clung to the sloping deck.

Macready's hands gripped the corded wheel firmly, coaxing, guiding the boat he knew so well. But the wind and the sea seemed determined to wrest the craft from his control, to throw him and his crew into the depths that it took all Macready's strength, both physical and mental, all his years of experience, all his instinctive feel for his boat to hold her steady and bring her inch by uncertain inch to the side of the crippled ship.

With supreme confidence in their coxswain, the lifeboat crew waited calmly, without a hint of fear on their faces, until he had manoeuvred the boat into the right position.

Only Fred Douglas, the second coxswain, glanced at Macready from time to time, just to be certain he was not needed to assist at the wheel.

The wind hammered at their ears, the salt lashed their eyes and stung their cheeks. There could be no word of command because of the noise of the storm and the ocean. The rescue would be conducted because each man knew his job so thoroughly.

Only young Tim Matthews on his first service kept his eyes darting from one to the other of his senior crew colleagues, anxious not to miss a signalled command, determined to do the right thing at the right time. So long he had waited for this moment and now it was here his only fear was not of the danger but of his failure to do what was expected of him.

Above them, as they moved in towards the ship, audible even over the lashing rain and blustering wind, was the pistol crack of a snapping cable and the rumble of shifting timber.

'Bloody 'ell,' Fred Douglas muttered. 'That lot's gonna come down on top of us!'

But Macready slammed the controls to full astern and the rudder, chewing at the foaming water, inched the boat away from the ship.

Briefly he saw the agonised expressions on the faces of the desperate crew above him. They thought he was leaving them.

Another cable snapped and two of the remaining packages of timber came hurtling down the slanting deck and into the water. The sea heaved, bringing the stricken vessel nearer to the retreating lifeboat. Another package rolled loose, teetered on the edge of the shifting deck and then toppled into the water dangerously close to the Oakley. Then a fourth rolled off, catching the bows of the lifeboat with a glancing blow making Chas Blake leap back smartly out of the way, swift enough to avoid injury but not quick enough to avoid a drenching from the spray as the heavy package splashed into the sea.

The lifeboatmen watched, waiting until all the loose timber had come away, but, frustratingly, one package slithered backwards and forwards across the deck, refusing to be pitched into the water. Macready waited a few minutes more, but all the time he was aware that the strength of the ship's crew, hanging desperately on to the side of the ship, was giving out.

They could not hold on much longer.

Falling timber from the listing ship or not, Macready knew he must go back in.

As he began to inch forward again, nearer and nearer the *Hroswitha*, even in this moment of crisis that demanded all his attention, refusing to be ignored, refusing to be clamped down, the ugly thought kept pushing its way to the forefront of his mind.

Where was Julie?

CHAPTER 17

The storm showed no sign of abating and Macready knew he had no choice but to attempt the rescue right now. Skilfully he manoeuvred the *Mary Martha Clamp* towards the *Hroswitha*, bringing the Oakley lifeboat almost under the listing starboard side of the ship.

Perilously close to the vessel, a huge wave brought the coaster towards the lifeboat with a lurch. The lifeboatmen did not waver from their stations but each and every man held his breath.

A collision seemed inevitable. The sides of the two boats touched and grated together and the crew braced themselves. Then miraculously the same wave that had pitched the *Hroswitha* towards them now carried the lifeboat forward and away from the looming coaster. Above them the three deckhands and the cook were on the point of exhaustion. Macready brought the lifeboat in again.

'Tim,' Macready bellowed above the roar of the sea and the wind. 'Get the loudhailer. Tell them as we go in when the boats touch to jump.'

Tim shouted the message through the loudhailer but the three men hanging by their arms gave no sign of having understood. The noise of the storm was such that they could probably not hear.

'Let's give it a try anyway,' Macready said.

On the port side of the lifeboat, four

crewmen stood with arms outstretched to grab the seamen as the lifeboat went in. The water beneath them swelled and the two vessels rose, first one and then the other, crashing together with more force this time, but at the moment of impact the three deckhands and the cook launched themselves towards the arms of the lifeboatmen. Three men landed relatively safely, with bruises and a twisted ankle, but they were aboard. The fourth—the deckhand who had injured his arm—jumped awkwardly, thudded against the outside of the lifeboat and slithered into the water. Tony Douglas had made a grab at him, but the man had slipped from his grasp.

'Man overboard!' Tony roared.

In these seas there were now two dangers for the man in the water. Being crushed between the lifeboat and the coaster or being sucked beneath the Oakley and cut to pieces by the propeller. Anxious faces peered over the side of the lifeboat as Macready at once thrust the control to stop.

A black head bobbed up in the small space of water between the two boats and a hand clutched at the empty air.

Tony unhooked the safety chain across the opening where they boarded the lifeboat at the launch and unfastened his own safety chain from the rail. He lowered himself down the scramble net.

'Watch out, Tony!' Alan Gilbert shouted a warning.

Tony glanced up and saw the vessel towering above them, a huge menacing bulk tossed mercilessly by the unlimited power of the heavy seas. The coaster heaved upwards on a wave and began to surge towards him, whilst the lifeboat unaffected as yet by the oncoming wave scarcely moved.

In that instant before the boats collided Tony bent down, crooked his arm and slid it beneath one of the seaman's armpits. The man clung on and Tony hauled him out of the water, every muscle in his body straining at the enormous effort. Alan leant over and grasped the Turk as Tony dragged him towards the scramble net and the sailor was pulled aboard.

'Quick, Tony. She's coming!'

The great ship lunged towards them as Macready rammed the control into full astern. Tony was up the nets and clambering on to the deck when the two boats clashed, trapping his left leg. He gave a howl of pain and then the lifeboat was borne away on the wave and by the thrust of its own engines. Tony collapsed on to the deck of the lifeboat. Alan and Tim carried him to the covered foredeck.

'Don't bother about me,' Tony gasped as Alan knelt and seemed about to pull off Tony's boot. 'Leave it. It'll be okay. Get back up there. Cox'n'll need you.'

'You sure, mate?'

Tony clenched his teeth against the pain, but he managed to nod and wave Alan away.

Tim weaved his way round the deck to the coxswain's cockpit. 'Mr Macready—Tony's hurt.'

'Aye, lad, I saw. Is it bad?'

'I dunno. But he won't let us do anything now.'

Macready nodded. 'Pete—radio the ship. Tell them we've got the four crew aboard the lifeboat. What about the Captain?'

Droysen's voice crackled over the airwaves. '...The Captain is ver' bad. The engineer has come up from below. He was concussed. Has injury on head, but is all right. Over.'

'Can they jump aboard like the deckies?'

Macready wanted to know.

There was a pause whilst some sort of consultation went on aboard the *Hroswitha*. Then the First Mate replied, 'The Captain cannot walk. The engineer will attempt the jump.'

'Right, Pete, tell the First Mate we'll take the Captain off next if the engineer can help the First Mate take on a breeches buoy. Then we'll take the engineer and the First Mate last.'

Droysen's reply was, 'Thank you, Cox-swain, but I shall be staying aboard the *Hroswitha* in the Captain's place.'

Macready grunted. He would get the others off first and then maybe argue that one out with the First Mate. He could sympathise with their unwillingness to abandon the ship entirely if there was a reasonable hope of being able to ride out the storm. No Captain or First Mate liked to see his ship pass into the hands of the salvage men. And yet, when life was at stake...

Macready now manoeuvred the *Mary Martha Clamp* into a position a short distance from the ship so that his bowman —Chas Blake in place of the absent Phil Davis—could fire the rocket carrying the thin line to the stricken vessel. Macready's voice was calm and his hands steady on the wheel, giving no outward indication of the agony in his mind, as, now in the position he wanted, he gave the order 'Let go anchor.'

Chas Blake fired the rocket. The line snaked towards the *Hroswitha* but a gust of wind caught it and tossed it carelessly off course and into the water. Chas prepared to make another attempt whilst the lifeboat coxswain concentrated on keeping the Oakley steady in the raging seas.

Julie, Julie, *Julie!* The name hammered through his mind and her face floated before his mind's eye. Macready clenched his jaw and watched his bowman's second attempt to fire the line across the intervening space. This time the line fell on to the ship but before Droysen, slithering about on the still sloping deck, could grab it, it slipped off and splashed into the sea.

On the third attempt there was a momentary lull in the wind and the line flew high above the ship and wrapped itself round one of the derricks. The lifeboat crew watched as Droysen struggled towards the line and began to haul on it. Across the space went the thicker rope which would carry the breeches-buoy. This Droysen secured to the base of the derrick which was leaning out from the listing ship towards the lifeboat at an angle of about thirty degrees. Then the German First Mate disappeared, climbing the ladder back to the bridge.

Now that the *Mary Martha Clamp* was attached to the stricken ship by the breeches-buoy line, the danger to the lifeboat was even greater. Anchored, she could not move away if the ship suddenly lunged towards her, and all eyes watched anxiously as Droysen reappeared with the engineer and between them they half-carried, half-dragged, the huge, almost limp figure of the Captain. Like three drunks, they staggered across the deck, slipping and sliding on the wet sloping surface. They reached the derrick and Macready watched as the First Mate and the engineer propped the sick man against the crane while they prepared to receive the sling of the breeches-buoy which the lifeboatmen now sent across. It took fifteen minutes of struggling to get the helpless man into the sling and by that time, Macready could see—even across the distance that separated them—that the injured engineer and the First Mate who seemed to be carrying all the responsibility, were themselves exhausted. At last they got the heavy man secure in the sling and signalled that they were ready.

The German Captain was winched across the boiling seas beneath. As the waves relentlessly buffeted the damaged coaster and the tiny lifeboat, it seemed an eternity that the man was being hauled across the space. First the line would go slack as the coaster was borne towards them and the sick man dangled only inches above the water. Then as that same wave hit the lifeboat, the line was stretched taut, almost to breaking-point. Inch by inch the man was drawn closer and willing hands reached out towards him to help him aboard the lifeboat whilst anxious eyes still watched the heaving coaster only a few yards away now.

A wave bigger than the rest rolled towards them, sweeping the cargo ship towards the lifeboat, just as the sling came over the side of the lifeboat and Schlick was set down.

The coaster bore down on them.

'Cut the cable,' Macready roared. 'Weigh anchor.'

The lifeboat's engines throbbed into renewed life, the anchor was hauled clear of the water but nearer and nearer came the huge ship.

In that split second before impact, Chas Blake wielded the axe and the rope between the two boats was severed in two. The lifeboat, full astern, thrust herself through the water away from the ship.

Now there remained only the First Mate and the engineer on board the *Hroswitha*.

Macready glanced at the echo sounder and saw that he only had about six feet draught. With each huge wave the helpless cargo ship was being pushed, bows foremost, nearer and nearer the sandbank.

'Pete, call up the coaster. Tell the First Mate if we don't take him and the engineer off now, they'll be on the sandbank. I presume he knows that,' Macready added, a little doubtful of the First Mate's condition considering all that had occurred during the last half an hour.

A few moments later Pete was reporting

back. 'He says he and the engineer want to stay aboard.'

Macready shrugged, but said, 'Tell him we'll stand by.'

Macready pulled the lifeboat back away from the *Hroswitha* to a distance of about a hundred yards. He was hardly able to relax even now, but at least for the time being the pressure had eased a little—at least the pressure of this particular service.

Now he had more time to think and the agonising thoughts crowded into his head.

Julie. Was there still no word? Surely Jack would have sent word if they had been found? He doubted that the inshore boat would have been able to launch in these seas, though he knew the reserve crew would try if there was any chance at all.

In the comparative lull, Macready said, 'Pete. Call up Jack and see if there's any news of—Julie.'

Unusually solemn-faced, Pete nodded.

The reply came through a few moments later and Pete repeated the gist of the message to Macready. 'They have reported the sailing-dinghy *Nerissa* as missing. Sandy says the car which towed the boat is still on Beach Road with the empty trailer. Jack's been back to search at Dolan's Point again, but they're not there. They must have put back to sea, probably before the weather deteriorated rapidly. Breymouth have been requested to ask for helicopter assistance as soon as available, but they got the same answer as us—not available at present. The ILB will attempt a launch...' Pete shrugged and turned back towards his radio, unable to bear the look on the big man's face.

Grimly Macready received the message in silence. He knew that the chances of the inshore lifeboat even being able to launch in such seas were virtually nil, though he knew the inshore lads would have a real try.

He knew also that the sailing-dinghy—new and sparkling though she might have been this morning—could be reduced to matchwood in minutes in such heavy seas.

Macready kept his hands firmly on the helm of the lifeboat, his gaze still upon the German coaster. By his side he felt, rather than saw, young Tim standing at his elbow.

He had overheard every word of the dreadful message.

CHAPTER 18

Relentlessly the wind, which had veered to north-west, pushed the helpless coaster towards Middle Bank, helped by the tide which had turned and was now flowing into the Wash. Nearer and nearer until finally, as if indeed this were the very aim, the waters surged up into one huge wave bearing the ship aloft and carrying it on to the sandbank. The vessel shuddered and creaked, the derricks rocked and swayed and the whole structure settled on to the sand, still tilting toward the starboard side. The cargo slithered around the deck, crashing into the superstructure, splashing into the water.

Dimly, through the glass screen of the wheelhouse, the lifeboatmen could see the two men still aboard tossed about like limp rag dolls.

'She's starting to break up. Now they'll have to come off,' Macready muttered and instructed Pete to call up the *Hroswitha* once more.

'*Hroswitha,* this is Saltershaven lifeboat. Suggest you abandon ship. We think she is starting to break up. Over.'

For a time there was no reply except the crackling over the airwaves. Then the voice of the First Mate was heard weakly. 'What's happened? Lifeboat—what's happened?'

Pete turned to Macready. 'I reckon he must have been thrown about. Sounds confused.'

'Explain what's happened. We canna do any more. It's a salvage job now.'

'*Hroswitha,* this is Saltershaven lifeboat. Your ship has been driven on to the sandbank. Coxswain suggests you let us take you off. Please acknowledge. Over.'

Again there was only interference and the noise of the wind and the sea whilst Macready and his radio/telephone operator waited.

Fred Douglas moved along the deck. 'Mac—we've done what we can for the survivors. But that Captain—he's in a bad way.'

'Right. Pete, tell the First Mate that his Captain needs immediate hospitalisation. He must realise that surely.'

Pete Donaldson repeated the message into the telephone. Faintly, Droysen's voice came over. 'Lifeboat, lifeboat. Take us off.'

'Tell him we're coming in. Be ready to jump.'

They saw the engineer and the First Mate emerge from the bridge, clinging to the handrails they slithered down the ladder and clawed at any handhold they could find as they slid down the deck towards the starboard rail.

Macready now approached the *Hroswitha* stern first. Nearer and nearer the sandbank until the propellers were churning into the loose sand and the echo sounder was showing no draught beneath the hull of the lifeboat. Closer, closer, inch by inch, and the engineer and the First Mate were hanging over the rail, waiting.

The first time the lifeboat came close enough for the engineer to try a jump across the intervening space, the man lost his nerve. His hands seemed frozen to the handrail, his eyes glazed with terror, the blood from a gash on his forehead smeared across his face by the rain and the sea spray.

They were within eight feet of the side of the huge hull above them. Fred, his eyes now on the echo sounder to assist

Macready, shouted a warning, even as they heard the engine shudder as the propellers were fouled by the sand. Macready pushed the controls to ahead slow and the lifeboat ploughed her way out of the sand and came away from the ship a little. As the gap widened between the two vessels, the engineer seemed to realise that he had missed his chance and looked as if he were about to attempt to jump the ever-increasing gap between himself and the lifeboat.

Gesticulating wildly, Chas Blake yelled at the German, 'No, no. Wait, man, wait!'

Once more, with infinite patience and gentleness, the coxswain put the controls into astern slow, but they could get no nearer, even though the *Hroswitha,* embedded in the sand, was now safer than she had been drifting at the mercy of the seas. Now she was held, she was not so much of a threat to the lifeboat. But still Macready could not reverse the Oakley near enough for the men to jump.

'Chas,' Macready shouted, 'get ready to fire a line up. We canna get close enough for them to jump.'

Once more the lifeboat went in and Chas

fired a line which snaked up and wrapped itself over the deck rail. Both men made a grab for it and hauled a thicker rope aboard. They fastened this to the foot of the derrick and Chas secured his end to the stern of the lifeboat. The engineer was first down the rope, swaying above the seas he came down steadily, hand over hand, sliding down towards the box at the stern of the Oakley. Chas and Fred Douglas reached out to catch him as his feet touched the lifeboat.

Macready fought the controls for now it was the lifeboat which was in danger of being driven on to the sandbank and becoming embedded alongside the coaster.

The First Mate was on his way down. A wave swept in and pushed the lifeboat towards the coaster so that the rope slackened and the man on the rope was dipped downwards towards the water. He clung on as Macready eased the Oakley forward and the rope tightened again.

'Come on, man, come on,' Fred Douglas called encouragingly. 'All we need now is for him to panic and not be able to move,' he added in a low voice.

'Shut up, Fred,' Chas muttered through

his teeth, his eyes still on the figure swinging over the water. But his words were spoken without malice and even in the seriousness of the moment, Fred grinned at being chided by his colleague for his fleeting pessimism.

Droysen was moving again, slithering down the last few feet of the rope, ignoring the burns on his hands in his desperate effort to reach the safety of the rescue boat. The instant his feet touched the deck, Chas raised the axe and cut the rope and Macready pushed the controls to full ahead and the lifeboat's propellers churned the loose sand and thrust the boat forward away from the sandbank.

As the *Mary Martha Clamp* drew away, Droysen stood at the stern of the lifeboat taking a last look at the stranded *Hroswitha*.

Pete Donaldson was speaking into his radio/telephone. During the actual rescue there had been radio silence, but now he had to report to headquarters. 'Breymouth coastguard, this is Saltershaven lifeboat. Do you read me? Over.'

'Saltershaven lifeboat, this is Breymouth coastguard. Go ahead. Over.'

'Breymouth coastguard, this is Salters-haven lifeboat. Service completed. The coaster *Hroswitha* is now aground on Middle Bank. We have all survivors aboard the lifeboat. One is in urgent need of hospital treatment. Two others are injured and a member of the lifeboat crew has a leg injury sustained during the rescue. Request helicopter assistance, immediate, if now available. Over.'

'Saltershaven lifeboat, this is Breymouth coastguard. Message received and under-stood. Rescue helicopter still not available. Suggest you beach at Saltershaven. Will arrange for local coastguard and ambulance to meet you there. Please report ETA. Over.'

'...Roger, Breymouth. ETA—eighteen forty-five. Out.'

A few seconds later, Jack Hansard's voice came over the radio link. 'Saltershaven lifeboat, this is Saltershaven coastguard. Message copied. Out.'

Then there was silence. A silence Macready did not want.

He was almost willing Jack Hansard to send a message that Julie and Howard had been found safely. But as the coxswain headed the lifeboat towards Saltershaven, the radio/telephone remained ominously silent.

The depression moved on north-eastwards across the North Sea, and with a cruel irony the gale-force winds were decreasing and the twenty-five-foot waves lessening as the lifeboat sped homewards.

Now they were approaching the area where the sailing-dinghy might be. Without a word being spoken, without even command or request from Macready, the lifeboatmen took up their look-out stations once more—all except the injured Tony Douglas and Alan Gilbert busy administering first aid to the survivors.

But Macready could not slow down to search now. He must beach at Saltershaven as soon as possible for the sake of the German Captain, who was now, Alan Gilbert had reported, in grave pain and slipping into unconsciousness every so often.

No—Macready could not stop to look for his daughter and the dilemma tore at his heart. He knew his duty and he would do it, but the decision crucified him.

The R/T crackled into life.

'Saltershaven lifeboat, this is Breymouth

coastguard. Do you read? Over.'

Pete replied at once, '...Loud and clear. Over.'

'...What is your position, please? Over.'

'...We are approaching Saltershaven Middle. Ten minutes to beaching. Over.'

'Saltershaven lifeboat, this is Breymouth coastguard. Confirm ambulance is now awaiting your arrival at Saltershaven beach. Over.'

'Breymouth coastguard, this is Saltershaven lifeboat. Roger and out.'

Then Jack Hansard's steady voice was heard. 'Saltershaven lifeboat, this Saltershaven coastguard. Message copied. Further message follows. Reference the sailing-dinghy reported missing probably off the Haven area: the inshore boat has attempted a launch. Conditions too severe. Will coxswain be able to undertake search as soon as survivors from coaster have been landed? Over.'

Pete turned worried eyes towards his coxswain. 'Did you hear that, Mac? Is it—Julie?'

Macready, his hands as steady as ever, his concentration never faltering from the task of weaving the lifeboat through the shoals, nodded. All he said was, 'Reply

287

affirmative.' Then he asked, 'Ask Jack to warn Jeff Caldicott—' Macready referred to one of the launchers who was also a reserve member of the crew—'to be ready to take Tony's place on the next service.'

They beached at twelve minutes to seven. The launching party were ready to receive the lifeboat but they all knew now that it was to go straight out again. Jack Hansard's landrover bounced across the sands, splashed through the creek towards the lifeboat already being hauled up on to the hard sand. Swiftly he ferried the sick Captain, the injured engineer and the deckhand and Tony Douglas to the ambulance waiting at the end of Beach Road. On the final run he took the rest of the crew of the German coaster up the beach.

Before he left the lifeboat Droysen shook Macready by the hand. There were tears in the young man's eyes as he said, 'Thank you. Thank you—for my life.'

Macready nodded and patted the grateful man on the shoulder, but his mind was already on the next service. And yet now that the moment had come when at last he could re-launch and head at full throttle towards the area where it was anticipated the sailing-dinghy might be, Macready felt a strange reluctance borne of fear.

He was desperately afraid of what he might find.

Ever since the moment when Sandy had spoken to him on the beach, in his heart of hearts Macready had longed to go in search of his daughter. But duty had kept him bound to the service of the moment—the stricken coaster.

But now? Now was a different matter entirely Macready knew that Julie—daughter of Saltershaven's lifeboat coxswain—would have by this time let the coastguard know that she and her companion were safe—if she had been able to do so.

Now, more than ever, he knew she was still somewhere out at sea.

The *Mary Martha Clamp* was hauled up on to the carriage, the launchers panting hard as they rushed the skeats from stern to bows. The safety chains were fastened, the tractor re-coupled and the carriage was turned right round so that the lifeboat once more faced out to sea. The crew, tired and windblown, climbed aboard again. Macready, standing on the deck near the top of the ladder spoke to Jeff Caldicott as he climbed up. 'Put a life-jacket on as soon as you come aboard.'

Macready fastened the chain across the opening and the tractor began to push the carriage into the water. The sea was still rough, but nothing like the conditions of three hours or so ago. The depression drifted on leaving destruction, and possibly even death, in its wake.

Macready blew his whistle, the chains were released and the tractor driver operated the launching gear. With a mighty splash, the spray fanning into the air, the lifeboat entered the water once more.

Macready headed out beyond Salters-haven Middle and then turned south-westwards to bring him back once more towards the shore, towards Dolan's Point, as Pete once more called up the Breymouth Coastal Rescue Headquarters to report this second launch and the change in the crew list.

Already the crew had taken up their look-out positions. Each and every one of them was grim-faced, their tired eyes scanning the rise and fall of the seas. Tim, standing in the bows next to Chas Blake, leaned forward, desperation in his young eyes. Macready, watching him, recognised the lad's anguish—it was the same as his own.

CHAPTER 19

They found him floating face downwards, his unresisting body tossed and buffeted by the choppy seas.

It was the worst moment of Macready's entire life as he fought to hold the lifeboat steady so that his crew could pluck Howard from the water.

The previous tragedies in Macready's life—the loss of his Scottish grandmother and consequently of his home too in the ravages of war, the death of his wife; everything paled into insignificance beside the fear gnawing at his guts.

Julie—Julie—*Julie!* The name hammered at his mind and for a moment his whole being seemed frozen, his own body lifeless, as if his life's blood had drained away.

Two members of the crew, Alan Gilbert and Chas Blake were working methodically yet speedily on the young man now lying under the tarpaulin covering the forward cockpit. Swiftly efficient, Alan wiped the mucus from Howard's white and wrinkled face, cleared his throat clogged with thick vomit and expelled water from his lungs. Then he turned Howard over and gave mouth to mouth resuscitation and applied the Brook Airway.

There was no response.

There was no pulse, no heartbeat, no warmth in any part of the young man's body.

After thirty minutes of effort, Alan sadly closed Howard's staring eyes and gagging mouth.

Macready saw young Tim stumble from the bows towards him. 'Cox'n—they...' His voice was choked with tears, not if he were truthful for Howard, but for Julie. 'They reckon—they can't do anything.' Tim's eyes mirrored the torture in Macready's own, but the lad's words, instead of plunging Macready into deeper despair, seemed strangely to break the bonds of inertia, seemed to bring back to Macready in that moment the realisation of what he was and who he was.

Years of experience and his ingrained

sense of duty were his salvation. With a brisk, yet not unkindly, nod, he acknowledged Tim's message and motioned to the lad that he should return to his look-out position. Activity and responsibility forced the agony to the back of his mind. It was there and whatever the outcome he knew he would relive these next few minutes, maybe hours, countless times in his nightmares, but for the present, he was coxswain of the lifeboat on a service—first and always.

The search had been going on even whilst Alan and Chas worked on Howard. At last Macready saw the two crew members emerge from the canopied bows and Alan weaved his way along the tossing deck towards his coxswain. Mutely, he shook his head, words in the noise of the wind and the driving seas, unnecessary.

Macready knew what he meant.

They could not revive Howard Marshall-Smythe.

The search continued, the lifeboat zigzagging backwards and forwards, all eyes scanning the seas as the searchlight swept back and forth across the surface of the water in the now fading daylight. She must be here somewhere. She would have her life-jacket on even if she had not be able to stay with the boat. The argument went on relentlessly inside Macready's head. But how could a young girl survive in such seas as they had experienced these last few hours?

Pete Donaldson was hunched over the radar screen. Suddenly he shouted, 'There's something in the water three degrees to port about half a mile away, Mac.'

Macready adjusted his course bearing and increased the speed and in minutes they were closing in on the object.

'There. *There!*' The wind, still gusting with intermittent strength, snatched the words from Tim's mouth and tossed them disdainfully away, but Macready and the rest of the crew saw him pointing.

They came alongside the capsized sailing-dinghy.

Julie was spread-eagled across the upturned hull.

Tim was over the side and down the scrambling net before anyone else had moved, leaning out to reach her. Chas went down after him and together they lifted her gently—so carefully—up into the lifeboat. Alan and Fred received her and carried her tenderly forward to the cockpit where the body of Howard Marshall-Smythe lay, now covered completely with a plastic sheet.

From his station at the wheel, Macready could not see whether Julie was alive or not. For a few moments Macready leant against the wheel, allowing his lifeboat to drift with the swell of the ocean.

He felt a hand on his shoulder. Fred Douglas was at his elbow. 'Let me tek over, Cox'n. You go for'ard to yon lass.'

'Aye, aye.' Macready relinquished the helm, easing his stiff fingers from the wheel, only now realising how tightly he had been gripping it.

Fred turned the *Mary Martha Clamp* towards Saltershaven. As Macready eased his way towards the foredeck, ironically the seas grew calmer with every minute.

He lifted the tarpaulin and squeezed himself beneath. He could see Julie lying on a stretcher already wrapped in blankets and a plastic sheet. Her head was cradled in Tim's arms, the young man bending over her anxiously, his body so positioned as if to shield the shrouded figure of her sailing companion from her.

Her face was wrinkled and swollen, her mouth cracked and bleeding, and she was so still.

Macready squatted down beside her scarcely able to breathe for the fear in his chest like a crushing weight.

Her swollen eyelids flickered and painfully she opened her eyes. Her sore lips moved and yet no sound came, then hoarsely she whispered, 'I knew you'd come!' She stretched out her fingers, blue with cold, towards her father.

Macready took her hand and pressed his rough, weathered cheek against it, the thankfulness rushing through him like a spring tide at the flood.

Tim turned to look into Macready's face, not ashamed of the tears running down his face as he asked, 'She'll be all right, won't she, Mr Macready?'

Macready's strong hand gripped Tim's shoulder. 'Aye, son, she'll be fine, she'll be fine.'

For years to come, Macready's sleep would be broken by nightmares. He would be haunted by the face of Howard Marshall-Smythe—the life they had not been able to save—and he would wake with a start in the depth of night not knowing, in those first few seconds, whether he had reached Julie in time.

Humbly Macready acknowledged the risk that duty had obliged him to take, the awful decision he had had to make.

He had gambled the precious life of his daughter against the power of the ocean.

The sea had not failed him. She had shown him her power over those who dared to treat her with disdain; she had taken the life of Howard Marshall-Smythe.

But the sea that Macready had always loved had given him back his daughter.

The publishers hope that this book has given you enjoyable reading. Large Print Books are especially designed to be as easy to see and hold as possible. If you wish a complete list of our books, please ask at your local library or write directly to: Magna Print Books, Long Preston, North Yorkshire, BD23 4ND, England.

This Large Print Book for the Partially sighted, who cannot read normal print, is published under the auspices of

THE ULVERSCROFT FOUNDATION

THE ULVERSCROFT FOUNDATION

. . . we hope that you have enjoyed this Large Print Book. Please think for a moment about those people who have worse eyesight problems than you . . . and are unable to even read or enjoy Large Print, without great difficulty.

You can help them by sending a donation, large or small to:

**The Ulverscroft Foundation,
1, The Green, Bradgate Road,
Anstey, Leicestershire, LE7 7FU,
England.**

or request a copy of our brochure for more details.

The Foundation will use all your help to assist those people who are handicapped by various sight problems and need special attention.

Thank you very much for your help.

Other MAGNA Mystery Titles In Large Print

WILLIAM HAGGARD
The Vendettists

C. F. ROE
Death By Fire

MARJORIE ECCLES
Cast A Cold Eye

KEITH MILES
Bullet Hole

PAULINE G. WINSLOW
A Cry In The City

DEAN KOONTZ
Watchers

KEN McCLURE
Pestilence